# Kate Hewitt

—

## ENGAGED FOR HER ENEMY'S HEIR

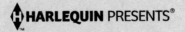

HARLEQUIN PRESENTS®

Recycling programs
for this product may
not exist in your area.

ISBN-13: 978-0-373-21370-2

Engaged for Her Enemy's Heir

First North American publication 2017

Copyright © 2017 by Kate Hewitt

Printed in U.S.A.

**"You are so beautiful. So lovely."
With gentle hands Rafael pushed her
disordered curls away from her face,
his fingers skimming across her skin,
exploring her features. Allegra closed
her eyes, submitting to his touch,
reveling in it.**

He slid his hands lower, each touch a question, his fingers feeling her collarbone and then his palm molding to the curve of her breast.

"A different kind of music," he murmured, his mouth following the trail of his hand, and she laughed, the sound shaky and breathless. Yes, this was new music, and he was teaching her its breathtaking melody. She'd thought, in this moment, that she might feel fear, or at least uncertainty, but she didn't.

She felt wonderful, and she wanted to keep feeling wonderful, to come alive under someone's hands, feel as close to another person as she could. For one night. One moment. When would she ever get a chance like this again?

Somehow Rafael had managed to slip her dress from her shoulders, and now her upper half was bare to him. He bent his head, nudging aside her bra with his tongue, and she gasped aloud, the feel of him against her sensitized flesh a jolt to her whole body.

"Oh..." The single syllable held a world of newly gained knowledge as pleasure pierced her with sweet arrows. Her hands roved over his back, drawing him closer to her, desire an insistent pulse inside her.

Of their own accord her hips rose, welcoming the knowing touch of his hand. His fingers brushed her underwear and she bit off a gasp. *She'd had no idea...*

# One Night With Consequences

*When one night...leads to pregnancy!*

When succumbing to a night of unbridled desire, it's impossible to think past the morning after!

But with the sheets barely settled, that little blue line appears on the pregnancy test and it doesn't take long to realize that one night of white-hot passion has turned into a lifetime of consequences!

Only one question remains:

How do you tell a man you've just met that you're about to share more than just his bed?

Find out in:

Look for more **One Night With Consequences** stories coming soon!

After spending three years as a die-hard New Yorker, **Kate Hewitt** now lives in a small village in the English Lake District with her husband, their five children and a Golden Retriever. In addition to writing intensely emotional stories, she loves reading, baking and playing chess with her son—she has yet to win against him, but she continues to try. Learn more about Kate at kate-hewitt.com.

### Books by Kate Hewitt

### Harlequin Presents

*Moretti's Marriage Command*
*Inherited by Ferranti*

### Seduced by a Sheikh

*The Secret Heir of Alazar*
*The Forced Bride of Alazar*

### The Billionaire's Legacy

*A Di Sione for the Greek's Pleasur*

### Secret Heirs of Billionaires

*Demetriou Demands His Child*

### One Night With Consequences

*Larenzo's Christmas Baby*

### The Marakaios Brides

*The Marakaios Marriage*
*The Marakaios Baby*

### The Chatsfield

*Virgin's Sweet Rebellion*

### Rivals to the Crown of Kadar

*Captured by the Sheikh*
*Commanded by the Sheikh*

Visit the Author Profile page at Harlequin.com for more titles.

To my lovely editor, Victoria. Thank you
for all your help with this one!

# CHAPTER ONE

IT SEEMED AS if a funeral was just a chance for people to get drunk. Not that Allegra Wells had personal experience of such a thing. She'd stuck to sparkling water all evening and now stood on the sidelines of the opulent hotel ballroom in Rome where her father's wake was being held and watched people booze it up. She could have felt bitter, or at least cynical, but all she could dredge up was a bone-aching, heart-deep weariness.

It shouldn't be this way.

Fifteen years ago it wouldn't have been.

She took a slug of water, half wishing it was alcohol that would burn its way down to her belly and make her finally feel something. Melt the ice she'd encased herself in for so long, so that numbness had become familiar, comforting. She didn't even notice it most of the time, content with her life back in New York, small as it was. It was only now, surrounded by strangers and with her father dead, that she felt painfully conscious of her isolation in the world she'd always viewed at a safe distance. The father who had turned his back on her without a thought.

Her father's second wife and stepdaughter Allegra knew, at least by sight. She'd never met them but she'd seen photos when, in moments of emotional weakness, she'd done an Internet search on her father. Alberto Mancini, CEO of Mancini Technologies. He was in the online tabloids often enough, because his second wife was young and socially ambitious—at least she seemed to be, from everything Allegra had seen and read online.

Her behaviour at the funeral, wearing black lace and dabbing her eyes with artful elegance, didn't make Allegra think otherwise. She hadn't spared Allegra so much as a glance, but then why would she? No one knew who Allegra was; she'd only known about the funeral because her father's lawyer had contacted her.

Around her people swirled and chatted, caught up in their own intricate dance of social niceties. Allegra wondered why she stayed. What she was hoping to find here? What did she think she could gain? Her father was dead, but he'd been dead to her for fifteen years, or at least she'd been dead to him. No messages, no letters or texts or calls in all that time. Nothing, and that was what she grieved for now, not the man himself.

The father she'd lost a long time ago, whose death now made her remember and ache for all she'd missed out on over the years. Was that why she'd come? To find some sort of closure? To make sense of all the pain?

Allegra's mother had been furious that she'd been attending, had seen it as a deep and personal betrayal. Just remembering Jennifer Wells's icy silence made Allegra's stomach cramp. Interactions with her mother were fraught at the best of times. Jennifer had never recovered from the way her husband had cut both her and Allegra out of his life, as neatly and completely as if he'd been wielding scissors. Although it hadn't felt neat. It had felt bloody and agonising, thrust from a life of luxury and indulgence into one of deprivation and loneliness, trying to make sense of the sudden changes, her father's absence, her mother's tight-lipped explanations that had actually explained nothing.

*'Your father decided our marriage was over. There's nothing I could do. He wants nothing to do with either of us any more. He won't give us a penny.'*

Just like that? Allegra had barely been able to believe it. Her father loved her. He swooped her up in her arms, he tickled her, called her his little flower. For years she had waited for him to call, text, write, anything. All she'd got, on and on, was silence.

And now she was here, and what was the point? Her father was gone, and no one here even knew who she was, or what she'd once been to him.

From across the room Allegra saw a flash of amber eyes, a wing of ink-black hair. A man was standing on the sidelines just as she was, on the other side of the room. Like her he was watching the crowds, and the look of contained emotion on his face echoed through Allegra, ringing a true, clear note.

She didn't recognise him, had no idea what he'd been to her father or why he was there— yet something in him, the way he held himself apart, the guarded look in his eyes, resonated with her. Made her wonder. Of course, she wouldn't talk to him. She'd always been shy, and her parents' divorce had made it worse. Chatting up a stranger at the best of times verged on impossible.

Still she watched him, covertly, although she doubted he noticed her all the way across the room, a pale, drab young woman dressed in fusty black with too much curly red hair. He, she realised, was definitely noticeable, and many women in the room were, like her, shooting him covert—and covetous—looks. He was devastatingly attractive, almost inappropriately masculine, his tall, muscular form radiating energy and virility in a way that seemed wrong at a funeral, and yet was seductively compelling.

They were here to commemorate death, and he was all life, from the blaze of his tawny eyes to the restless energy she felt in his form, the loosely clenched fists, the way he shifted his weight, like a boxer readying for a fight. She was drawn not just to his beauty but to his vitality, feeling the lack of it in herself. She felt drained and empty, had for a long time, and as for him…?

Who was he? And why was he here?

Taking a deep breath, Allegra turned and headed for the bar. Maybe she would have that drink after all. And then she would go back to the *pensione* where she'd booked a small room, and then to the reading of her father's will tomorrow, although she hardly thought he'd leave her anything. Then home to New York, and she'd finally put this whole sorry mess behind her. Move on in a way she only now realised she hadn't been able to.

She ordered a glass of red wine and retreated to a private alcove off the main reception room,

wanting to absent herself as much as she could
without actually leaving.

She took a sip of wine, enjoying the velvety
liquid and the way it slipped down her throat,
coating all the jagged edges she felt inside.

'Are you hiding?'

The voice, low, melodious, masculine, had
her tensing. She flicked her gaze up from the
depths of her glass and her eyes widened in
shock at the sight of the man in front of her.
*Him.*

It was as if she'd magicked him from her
mind, teleported him across the room to stand
here like a handsome prince from a fairy-tale,
except there was something a little too wicked
about the glint in his eye, something too hard
about the set of his mouth, for him to be the
prince of a story.

*Was he the villain?*

Too stunned to form a coherent response,
or one of any kind, Allegra simply stared. He
really was amazingly good-looking—dark
hair cut slightly, rakishly long, those glinting,
amber eyes, and a strong jaw with a hint of
sexy stubble. He was dressed in a dark grey
suit with a darker shirt and a silver-grey tie,
and he looked a little bit like Allegra imagined
Mephistopheles would look, all dark, barely
leashed power, the energy she'd felt from across

the room even more forceful now, and twice as compelling.

'Well?' The lilt in his voice was playful, yet with a dark undercurrent that snaked its way inside Allegra like a river of chocolate, pure sensual indulgence. 'Are you?'

Was she what? She was gaping, that much was certain. Allegra snapped her mouth closed and forced her expression into something suitably composed. She hoped.

'As a matter of fact, I am. Hiding, that is. I don't know anyone here.' She took a sip of wine, needing the fortification as well as the second's respite.

'Do you make a habit of crashing funerals?' he asked lightly, and she tensed, not wanting to admit who she was…the rejected daughter, the cast-off child, coming back for scraps.

"Not unless there's an open bar," she joked, hefting her glass, and the man eyed her thoughtfully. Did he believe her? She couldn't tell. 'Did you know him?' she asked. 'Alberto Mancini?' The name stuck in her throat, and she saw a flash in the stranger's eyes, a single blaze of feeling that she couldn't identify but which still jolted her like lightning.

'Not directly. My father did business with him, a long time ago. I wanted to…pay my respects.'

'I see.' She tried to gather her scattered wits. The look of sleepy speculation in the man's eyes made her skin prickle. His gaze was like a caress, invisible fingertips trailing on her heated skin. She'd never reacted to someone so viscerally before, so immediately. Maybe it was simply because her emotions were raw, everything too near the surface. She certainly couldn't ever recall feeling this way before. 'That's very kind of you.' He smiled and said nothing. 'What did you say your name was?'

'I didn't.' His gaze swooped over her again, like a hawk looking for its prey. 'But it's Rafael.'

Rafael Vitali didn't know who this beguiling woman was, but he was captivated by her cloud of Titian curls, the wide, grey eyes that were as clear as mirrors, reflecting her emotions so he could read them from across the room. Weariness. Sorrow. *Grief.*

Who was she? And what was her relationship to Mancini? It didn't really matter, not now his business was done, justice finally satisfied, but he was still curious. A family friend—or something less innocuous? A lover? A mistress? She hadn't come just for the bar, of that he was certain. So what was she hiding?

Rafael took a sip of his drink, watching the emotions play across her face like ripples in water. Confusion, hope, sadness. A lover, he decided, although she was surely young enough to be his daughter. Mancini's wife and daughter were across the room, looking sulky and even bored. Rafael would have spared a second of sympathy for the man's widow if he hadn't known how she'd raced through his money. And tomorrow she would discover how little there was left…perfect justice, considering how Mancini had done the same to his mother, leaving her with nothing.

And as for his father…

He braced himself for the flash of pain, the memories he closed off as a matter of self-protection, of sanity. He never let himself think about his father, couldn't go to that dark, closed-off place, and yet for some reason Mancini's death had pried open that long-locked door, and now he was feeling flickers of the old pain, as raw as ever, like flashes of lightning inside him, a storm of emotion he needed to control.

*'Take care of them for me, Rafael. You're the man of the house now. You must protect your mother and sister. No matter what…'*

But, no. He needed to slam that door shut once more, and right now he knew the perfect way to do it…with this beguiling woman by his side.

'I hope the bar is worth enduring a wake for,' he said lightly, and she grimaced.

'I'm not really here for the bar.'

'I thought not.' He braced a shoulder against the wall so he was closer to her, inhaling her light, floral scent. A flyaway strand of coppery hair brushed his shoulder. She was utterly lovely, from her silver-grey eyes to her pert nose and lush mouth, her skin pale and creamy with a scattering of red-gold freckles. 'So how did you know him?' he asked.

She shrugged, her gaze sliding away. 'I knew him a long time ago. I'm not even sure he'd have remembered me, to be honest.' She let out a wavering laugh that sounded a little too sad, and Rafael resisted the tug of sympathy he felt for her. He didn't want to feel sorry for her, not now. Not when he'd already decided to sleep with her. Besides, she was no doubt been one of Mancini's cast-off mistresses, a gold-digger in it for the money and baubles. Why feel sorry for such a woman?

And yet he couldn't help but notice how fragile she looked, as if a breath might blow her away. There were violent smudges like bruises under her eyes, and her face was pale underneath the gold dust scattering of freckles. The figure underneath the rather shapeless black dress looked slender and willowy, with a hint of intriguing curves. 'I can't believe anyone would forget you,' he said, and was amused to see her cheeks turn pink, her pupils flare, as if she were an innocent unused to compliments.

'Well…you'd be surprised,' she returned with an uncertain laugh. 'What business did your father have with my—with him?'

'A new technology for mobile phones.' He didn't want to talk about the past. 'At least new at the time. The industry has moved on quite a bit since then.' But the technology would have made his father a lot of money, if Mancini hadn't cut him off. If he'd lived.

'I wouldn't know. I'm rather useless with technology. I can barely manage my own phone.' She took a sip of wine, golden-red lashes sweeping down onto her porcelain cheeks. Rafael had the desire, unsettlingly strong, to sweep his thumb along her cheek and see if her pale skin felt as creamily soft as it looked.

'What do you do, then?' he asked. 'For a living?' He reckoned she must be in her late twenties. Had she found a new sugar daddy?

'I work at a café, in Greenwich Village. It's a music café.'

'A music café? I've never heard of such a thing.'

'It's a shop for instruments and libretto,' Allegra explained. 'As well as a café. But it's so much more than that—it hosts concerts for aspiring musicians, and offers lessons to all sorts of people. It's a bit of a community hub, for music-lovers at least.'

'And you are one, I gather?'

'Yes.' Her voice was quiet and heartfelt, as well as a little bit sad. 'Yes, music is very important to me.'

Rafael watched her, disconcerted by this shy admission, by the genuineness of it, of her. He didn't want to confuse or complicate his feelings, had no intention of deepening what would be a shallow but satisfying sexual transaction.

'I suppose I should leave,' Allegra said slowly. 'I don't really have a reason to stay.' She sounded reluctant, and when she looked up at him her eyes were full of mute appeal, wanting him to stop her. And stop her he would.

'It's still early,' he said as he angled his body closer to her, his shoulder brushing hers, letting her feel both his heat and intent. Her eyes widened, and her tongue darted out to touch her lips. Primal need blazed through him. She was either artless or very, very experienced—he couldn't tell which, but either way she enflamed him. 'But we don't have to stay here. Tell me what your favourite piece of music is.'

'Oh…' She looked surprised, and then shyly pleased. 'I don't think you'd know it.'

'Try me.'

'All right.' She smiled, and it felt like a ray of sunlight on his soul, disconcertingly bright, reaching too many dark corners. It was just a *smile*. 'It's the third movement of the Cello Sonata by Shostakovich. Do you know it?'

'No, but I wish I did. I wish I could hear it.'

'He's not one of the most well-known composers, but his music is so emotional.' Her grey eyes developed a pearly sheen; she looked almost tearful. 'It moves me like nothing else does.'

'Now I really wish I could hear it.' The look of naked emotion on her face caught at him unexpectedly. He'd started the conversation about music as a way to invite her up to his suite, but now he found he genuinely wanted to hear the piece. 'I have a suite in this hotel,' he said. 'With an amazing sound system. Why don't you come upstairs and listen to the piece with me?'

Allegra's eyes widened with stunned comprehension. 'Oh, but…'

'We can have a proper drink at the same time. The bar up there is much better than the plonk they're serving down here.' He whisked her glass from her fingertips and deposited it on the tray of a hovering waiter. 'Come.' He held out his hand, willing her to agree. The evening couldn't end here, unsettled, unsated.

He needed more. He craved the connection and satisfaction he knew he'd find with her, however brief.

Allegra stared at his outstretched hand, her eyes wide, her fingers knotted together. 'I'm not...' she began, and then trailed off, looking endearingly uncertain. Was it an act? Or was she really reluctant?

He didn't want her reluctant. 'I am,' he said, and reached for her hand, pulling her gently towards him. She came slowly, with hesitant steps, her wide-eyed gaze searching his face, looking for reassurance.

And he gave it as his fingers closed around hers, encasing the spark that had leapt between them at the first brush of skin. He drew her by the hand, away from the circulating crowds. A few people gave them curious looks, a veiled glance of envy that Rafael ignored, just as he'd ignored the subtle and not so subtle come-ons of the various women there. There was only one he wanted, and he was holding her hand.

They walked hand in hand out of the room, across the foyer, and then to the bank of gleaming lifts. Rafael's heart started to race in expectation. He was looking forward to this more than he'd looked forward to anything in a long time.

He pressed the button for the lift, holding his

breath, not wanting to break the fragile spell that was weaving its way around both of them. Not wanting to let her entertain second thoughts.

The doors opened and they stepped inside, the lift thankfully empty. As the doors closed Rafael turned to her. 'You have the most enchanting smile.'

She looked completely surprised. 'Do I?' she asked, and he nodded, meaning it, because her smile *was* lovely, a shy, slow unfurling, like the petals of a flower. More and more he was thinking she was genuine, that her air of innocence and uncertainty wasn't an act. At least, not that much of an act. She must have had some experience, to be mourning Mancini, and yet she almost seemed untouched.

'You do. And I think it is a rare but precious thing.' He leaned back against the wall of the lift and tugged her gently towards him, close enough so their hips nudged each other's and heat flared, a spreading, honeyed warmth that left him craving more. 'I would like to see it more often.'

'We have been at a funeral,' Allegra murmured, her gaze sweeping downwards. 'There hasn't been much cause to smile.'

The doors pinged open before Rafael had to come up with a response to that thorny statement. He stepped out, directly into the penthouse suite he'd booked. Allegra looked around the soaring, open space, her eyes wide.

'This is amazing…'

Was she not used to such things? Rafael shrugged the question aside, drawing her deeper into the room. The doors to the lift closed. At last they were alone.

# CHAPTER TWO

*WHAT WAS SHE DOING?* Allegra felt as if she'd stumbled into an alternate reality. What kind of woman followed a strange, sexy man up to his penthouse suite? What kind of woman fell headlong under his magnetic spell?

Certainly not her. She didn't do anything unexpected or impetuous. She lived a quiet life, working at the café, her closest friend its owner, an eighty-year-old man who treated her like a granddaughter. Her life was small and safe, which was how she wanted it. And yet from the moment Rafael's hand had touched hers she'd been lost, or perhaps found. She felt as she'd been wired into a circuit board she'd had no idea existed, nerves and sensations springing to life, making her entire body tingle.

She *felt*, and after the numbness she'd encased herself in that was both good and painful, a necessary jolt, waking her up, reminding her she was alive and someone, *someone* was looking at her with warmth and even desire, wanting her to be there. The knowledge was intoxicating, overwhelming.

Rafael was still holding her hand, his warm, amber eyes on hers, his smile as slow and sensual as a river of honey trickling through her.

It was dangerous, letting herself be looked at like that. Dangerous and far too easy to float down that river, see where its seductive current took her. They were here to listen to music, but Allegra wasn't so naïve and inexperienced not to realise what that meant. Why Rafael had really asked her up here.

Nervous and unsettled by her spiralling thoughts, Allegra tugged her hand from Rafael's and walked around the suite, taking in all the luxurious details, soaring ceilings and marble floors, ornate woodwork and silk and satin cushions on the many sofas scattered around the large living area.

'This place really is incredible,' she said. Her voice sounded high and thin. 'What a view.' Floor-to-ceiling windows framed a spectacular view of the city on three sides. 'Is that the Coloseum?' She pointed blindly, and then felt Rafael come to stand behind her, his body so close she could feel his heat. If she stepped backwards so much as an inch she'd be touching him, burned by him. She wanted it, and yet she was afraid.

This was entirely new, and new meant unfamiliar. Strange. *Dangerous*.

Except…what, really, did she need to be afraid of? Rafael couldn't hurt her, not in the way she'd been hurt before, soul deep, heart shattered. She wouldn't let him. She was nervous, yes, because this was strange and new, but she didn't have to be *afraid*. She took a deep breath, the realisation calming her. She could be in control of this situation.

'Yes, it's the Coliseum.' His hands rested lightly on her shoulders, and a slight shudder went through her, which she knew he felt. Daring now to prolong the moment, to up the ante, she leaned back so she was resting lightly against him. The feel of his chest, hard and warm, against her back was a comforting, solid weight, grounding her in a way she hadn't expected. Making her want to stay there.

Rafael's hands tightened on her shoulders and they stood there for a moment, her back against his chest so they could feel each other's heartbeats. Allegra closed her eyes, savouring the moment, the connection. Because that's what she wanted, what she needed now…to feel connected to someone. To feel alive.

So much of her life had been lived alone, since she was too shy to make friends at school, too confused and hurt to reach out to her mother, too wounded and wary to seek love from the handful of dates she'd had over the years. But *this*...one single, blazing connection, to remind her she was alive and worth knowing...and then to walk away, unhurt, still safe.

'Shall we have champagne?' Rafael's voice was soft, melodious, and Allegra nodded. She wasn't much of a drinker, but she wanted to celebrate. Wanted to feel this was something worth celebrating.

'That sounds lovely.'

He moved away and she turned, wishing she could get hold of her galloping emotions, her racing pulse. Feeling this alive was both exquisite and painful. What was it about this man that made her want to take a step closer, instead of away? That made her want to risk after all this time?

The pop of a cork echoed through the room, making Allegra start. Rafael poured two glasses, careless of the bubbles that foamed onto the floor. *'Cin-cin,'* he murmured, a lazy look in his eyes, and he handed her a glass.

*'Cin-cin,'* Allegra returned. She hadn't spoken the informal Italian toast since she was twelve years old, and the memory was bittersweet. New Year's Eve at her family home, an estate in Abruzzi, snow-capped mountains ringing the property. Her father had given her her

first taste of champagne, the crisp bubbles tart and surprising on her tongue. The sense of happiness, like a bubble inside her, at being with her family, safe, secure, loved.

Had it all been a mirage? A lie? It must have been. Or perhaps she was remembering the moment differently, rose-tinted with the innocence of childhood, the longing of grief. Perhaps her father hadn't been as doting as she remembered; perhaps he'd taken a call moments after the toast, left her alone. How could she ever know? She couldn't even trust her memories.

'Are you going to drink?' Rafael asked, and Allegra blinked, startled out of her thoughts.

'Yes, of course.' She took a sip, and the taste was as crisp and delicious as she remembered. She blinked rapidly, wanting to clear the cobwebs of memory from her already overloaded mind. She didn't want to get emotional in front of a near-stranger.

'Tell me about yourself,' she said when she trusted herself to sound normal. 'What do you do?'

'I run my own company.'

She raised her eyebrows. 'What kind of company?'

'Property. Mainly commercial property, hotels, resorts, that sort of thing.'

He was rich, then, probably very rich. She

should have guessed, based simply on his presence, his confidence. Even his cologne, with the dark, sensual notes of saffron, smelled expensive. Privileged. She'd been privileged once too, before her parents' divorce. More privileged and even spoiled than she'd ever realised, until it had all been taken away.

Not that she'd been focused on her father's money. Although her mother complained bitterly that after the divorce she'd got nothing, that she'd had to scrounge and beg and pawn what jewellery she'd managed to keep, Allegra hadn't really cared about any of it. Yes, it had been a huge step down—from an enormous villa to a two-bedroom apartment too far uptown to be trendy, public school, no holidays, often living off the generosity of her mother's occasional boyfriends, a parade of suited men who came in and out of her mother's life, men Allegra had tried her best to avoid.

All of it had made her mother bitter and angry, but Allegra had missed her father's love more than any riches or luxuries. And at the same time she'd become determined never to rely on anyone for love or anything else ever again. People let you down, even, especially, the people closest to you. That was a lesson she didn't need to learn twice.

'And you enjoy what you do?' she asked Rafael. She felt the need to keep the conversation going, to avoid the look of blatant, sensual intent in his eyes. She wasn't ready to follow that look and see where it led, not yet, and Rafael seemed content to simply sip and watch her with a sleepy, heavy-lidded gaze.

'Very much so.' He put his half-full glass on a table and moved towards the complicated and expensive-looking sound system by the marble fireplace. 'Why don't we listen to your music? Shostakovich, you said, the third movement of the cello sonata?'

'Yes…' She was touched he'd remembered. 'But surely you don't have it on CD?'

He laughed softly. 'No, I'm afraid not. But the sound system is connected to the Internet.'

'Oh, right.' She laughed, embarrassed. 'Like I said, I'm not good with technology.'

'You can leave that to me. I can find it easily enough.' And he did, for within seconds the first melancholy strains of the music were floating through the room. Rafael turned to her, one hand outstretched, just as it had been before. 'Come.'

The music was already working its way into her soul, the soft strains winding around her, touching a place inside her no person ever accessed. Music was her friend, her father, her lover. She'd given it the place meant for people, for relationships, and she'd done that deliberately. Music didn't hurt you. It didn't walk away.

She took Rafael's hand, the sorrowful emotion of the cello resonating deep within her. Rafael drew her down onto the sumptuous leather sofa, wrapping one arm around her shoulders so she was leaning into him, breathing in his scent, her body nestled against his.

It was the closest she'd ever been to a man, and yet bizarrely the intimacy felt right, a natural extension of the music, the moment, both of them silent as the cello and piano built in sound and power.

Then Rafael drew her against him even more tightly, so her cheek was pressed against his chest, her body pressed against his, and Allegra closed her eyes, letting the music wash over her. She needed this. She closed her eyes, the music and Rafael and the champagne all combining to overwhelm her senses even as it made her want more, to let herself be swept away on this tide of emotion and see where it took her.

Underneath her cheek Rafael's chest rose and fell in steady, comforting breaths. His fingers stroked her arm and his breath feathered her hair. Everything about the moment felt incredibly intimate, more so than anything Allegra had ever experienced before. If only they could go on like this for ever, feeling each other's breaths, each beat of their hearts.

The music built to its desperate, haunting crescendo and then the strains fell away into silence. It had been, Allegra knew from having listened to the piece many times, just over eight minutes, and yet it felt like a lifetime. She felt both drained and intensely alive at the same time, and in the ensuing stillness neither of them moved or spoke.

'Do you know,' Allegra finally said softly, 'the cello is closest instrument to the human voice? I think that's why it affects me so much.' She let out a shaky laugh, conscious of the tears on her cheeks, the rawness of the moment. The music had affected her more now than it ever had before.

'It is a stunning piece of music,' Rafael said quietly. His thumb found her tear and gently swept it away, stealing her breath, making her ache. 'It causes me to both yearn and mourn.'

*'Yes...'* The sensitive, sincerely spoken observation pierced her to her core. *This* was the connection she craved, and unthinkingly she twisted in his arms, smiling through her tears, her face tilted up to his. Then she caught the blazing look in his eyes, felt its answer in the sudden, desperate thrill that rippled through her

body. And this connection, even sweeter and more powerful than the last…

He dipped his head and she held her breath, the whole world suspended, expectant—and then his mouth was covering hers in a kiss that felt like both a question and an answer, a need both sating and sparking to life. It was enough, and yet it made her want so much more.

Allegra's hands clenched on the crisp cotton of his shirt as his mouth moved with thorough and expert persuasion on hers, gentle and yet so sure. She'd never known a kiss could be like this, touching her to her very core, piercing her right through, *knowing* her. And right now she wanted to be known.

And then it became wonderfully, thrillingly more. In one easy movement Rafael swept her up and across the room and she found herself lying down on the soft leather cushions, his face flushed and his eyes jewel-bright as he looked down at her.

'You are so beautiful. So lovely.' With gentle hands he pushed her disordered curls away from her face, his fingers skimming across her skin, exploring her features. Allegra closed her eyes, submitting to his touch, revelling in it. The feel of his fingers on her face felt as intimate as the kiss, his touch so gentle and reverent it made her ache in an entirely new way.

He slid his hands lower, each touch a question, his fingers feeling her collarbone and then his palm moulding to the curve of her breast.

'A different kind of music,' he murmured, his mouth following the trail of his hand, and she laughed, the sound shaky and breathless. Yes, this was new music, and he was teaching her its breathtaking melody. She'd thought, in this moment, that she might feel fear, or at least uncertainty, but she didn't.

She felt wonderful, and she wanted to keep feeling wonderful, to come alive under someone's hands, feel as close to another person as she could. For one night. One moment. When would she ever get a chance like this again?

Somehow Rafael had managed to slip her dress from her shoulders, and now her upper half was bare to him. He bent his head, nudging aside her bra with his tongue, and she gasped aloud, the feel of him against her sensitised flesh a jolt to her whole body.

'Oh...' The single syllable held a world of newly gained knowledge as pleasure pierced her with sweet arrows. Her hands roved over his back, drawing him closer to her, desire an insistent pulse inside her.

Of their own accord her hips rose, welcoming the knowing touch of his hand. His fingers

brushed her underwear and she bit off a gasp.
*She'd had no idea...*

Rafael lifted his head, his gaze glittering as
he looked down at her, his breathing as ragged
as her own. The obvious fact that he wanted her
as much as he wanted him solidified her certainty that this was what she wanted. What she
needed. A connection, pure and true.

'Will you come into the bedroom with me?'

She nodded wordlessly, knowing there was
only one answer her aching body and heart
could give.

'Yes.'

In one fluid movement Rafael rose from the
sofa and drew her towards the bedroom. Allegra followed, barely conscious of her rucked-
up dress, her tangled hair.

The bedroom was as elegant and luxurious
as the living area, and Allegra glanced at the
massive king-sized bed, standing on its own
dais and covered in a navy satin duvet. Rafael
turned her to face him, framing her face with
his hands as he kissed her again, even more
deeply, and she responded, his kiss drawing a
deep, pure note from her soul.

Rafael tugged the zip down the back of her
dress so the black silk fell away, leaving her in
nothing but her bra and pants, both simple and
black, hardly sexy, and yet his gaze gleamed

with approval as he looked at her, and her heart swelled. She had never realised how wonderful it felt, to have a man look at her like that. Want her like that. He drew her towards him, her breasts brushing against his chest, her hips nudging his so she could feel the hard length of his arousal against her stomach.

'Cold?' he whispered, and she shook her head.

No, she was not cold. It was a balmy spring evening, and the hotel suite was warm. The shiver was because of him, and he knew it, and she didn't care.

He kissed her again, working his way down her jaw and collar bone to press his lips against the V between her breasts. She threaded her fingers through his hair, anchoring herself to him. She felt adrift in sensation, and his touch was the only thing that tethered her to earth.

Then he was moving his mouth lower, peeling away her bra and pants with his hands, sinking down onto his knees in front of her so Allegra swayed, shocked and overwhelmed by the feel of his hands on her hips, his *mouth*...

'Oh...' Her breath came out in shattered gasps. It was so unbearably intimate, to have him looking at the very essence of her, revering her in an act so selfless and giving and... *'Oh.'*

Rafael's dark chuckle reverberated through

her bones as her body trembled on the precipice of an orgasm that felt like an explosion. He rose again and drew her to the bed, leaving her trembling and aching and wanting more.

She watched, dazed, as he shucked off his clothes, revealing a bronzed torso, the muscles of his abdomen scored into hard, perfect ridges. His legs were long and powerful, and as for the most male part of him…

He was a work of beauty.

'You may look,' Rafael said as he covered her body with his. 'And you may also touch.' And then he was kissing her again, his arousal pressing into her with thrilling insistence, and that restless ache became an overwhelming clamour in her body, drowning out all thought, all doubt.

She gasped out loud as his fingers touched her in her most intimate and feminine places, teasing, toying, exploring, *knowing*. Her fingernails dug into the satiny skin of his shoulders as her body strained for the glittering apex she felt, just out of her reach, a pinnacle she needed to find, that she wanted them to ascend together.

And then, finally, he was sliding inside her, his breathing harsh and ragged as he filled her up, the momentary twinge of pain lost in the utter rightness of the sensation, the union complete and total.

He stopped, swearing under his breath, and,

lost in a haze of need, Allegra stilled underneath him.

'Rafael…?'

'You are *vergine*?' he demanded, and she gulped.

'Yes…'

He swore again, his forehead pressed to hers. 'I had no idea…'

'Why would you?' she managed, and he let out a shudder, his eyes clenched closed.

'You should have told me.'

'Rafael…' She arched her hips upwards, letting her body plead in a way her words could not. She couldn't let him stop now, not when everything in her was aching and demanding. With a groan he kept moving, the delicious slide of his body in hers making Allegra forget that tense moment as she gave herself up to the sensations cascading through her, building in a beautiful crescendo, and then the glittering apex burst into crystalline shards of pleasure around her as she let out a cry that rent the still air and then fell away like the most sacred note of music she'd ever heard.

Rafael rolled off Allegra, managing to suppress the curse that sprang to his lips once more. She'd been a *virgin*. He hadn't expected that, not even when he'd decided she was artless and genuine, and guilt soured like acid in his stomach. He'd stolen someone's innocence. He'd used someone who should have been protected, cared for. He'd done something he'd sworn he would never do again. Break a sacred trust.

He'd assumed she was a woman of some experience, even if she'd seemed a little shy. He never would have brought her upstairs otherwise. He never would have gone ahead with his seduction.

And yet…the music, the mood, the way Allegra had looked at him with hungry hope…all of it had made him yearn in a way that now left him feeling deeply uneasy. Sex was a transaction, nothing more, pleasurable and easy as it was. He didn't ever let it mean anything, and he hoped like hell Allegra wasn't imbuing it with some kind of emotion he would never let himself feel.

And yet it had been the innocent purity of her response that had been his undoing. *He hadn't even used birth control.* The realisation crystallised like ice inside him. He'd meant to reach for a condom, but in the moment he'd completely forgotten. He'd lost his head. He'd certainly lost control of his body.

Next to him Allegra was still, a rosy flush covering her pale, porcelain body, the perfect foil for the creaminess of her skin. Her hair was spread across the pillow in a tangle of red-gold curls, making him want to thread his fingers through them even now, and pull her towards him for an open-mouthed kiss. Even now, with his climax still thudding through him, knowing how innocent she'd been, he wanted her. He'd never wanted a woman so quickly, or so much.

Allegra rolled on her side, curling into him, her arms wrapped around his chest. Rafael froze, confusion colliding with alarm, irritation with guilt. He didn't do pillow talk. Ever. All of his bed partners knew what he expected in bed, and what he definitely didn't want. He made it very clear from the beginning that emotional attachments were a no-go zone, except Allegra, of course, hadn't received that memo. And as a virgin she would no doubt expect some intimacy now, some soft talk that he knew he was utterly incapable of. He didn't let people get close. People he could hurt. People he could fail.

As he'd already hurt Allegra, deflowering her in what amounted to a tawdry one-night stand.

Her leg found its way between his, her damp cheek pressed to his chest. She let out a shuddering sigh.

'I miss him,' she whispered, her voice sounding broken. 'I miss him so much.'

Shock had Rafael stilling. *What the hell...?*

'Miss him?' he repeated tonelessly.

'I know I shouldn't, there's nothing to miss,' she continued softly. 'I hadn't even seen him in fifteen years. But I do miss him. I miss what we once had, what I thought we had. That's why I came tonight, I think. Because I was looking for something, some kind of closure...'

She was talking about Mancini. But *fifteen years*... She couldn't have been his mistress. She was in her late twenties at most.

'Allegra,' Rafael asked hoarsely, turning to stare down into her pale, lovely face. 'Who are you?'

She looked up at him with tear-drenched eyes. 'I'm his daughter,' she said simply, and Rafael bit down on the curse that sprang to his lips.

Allegra was Alberto Mancini's *daughter*. The daughter of his enemy, his nemesis, was lying in his arms, seeking his comfort, because her dear father, the man who had as good as murdered his own, was dead.

His stomach heaved. He felt a thousand different emotions—fury and guilt, disgust and alarm, regret and sorrow. He was sickened by his own part in this unexpected drama, taking a woman's innocence, a woman who he should, by rights, have nothing to do with. He'd hated the Mancinis for so long, had wanted only justice...but what was this? What was *he*? Allegra was looking for comfort and he had none to give.

He rolled away from her and out of bed, grabbing his boxers and slipping them on in one jerky movement. From behind him he heard Allegra shift in bed, and then her voice, trembling, uncertain.

'Rafael?'

'You should go.' His voice was brusque; he didn't think he could have gentled it if he'd tried. Anger was coursing through him now, a pure, clean rage. Mancini's *daughter*. Did she know what her father had done? Did she realise the blood he had on his hands? Reasonably he knew she couldn't; she must have been a child when his own father had died.

And yet…she was a Mancini. She missed her father, a man he'd hated. She'd been innocent, and he'd abused it. His feelings were a confused tangle of guilt and anger, shame and frustration. It was all too much to deal with. He needed her out of his life. Immediately.

'You…you want me to go?' Her voice was a trembling breath of uncertainty.

'I'll call you a cab.' He reached for his trousers and pulled them on. Then, because she still wasn't moving, he grabbed her dress and tossed it to her. It fell on her lap; she didn't even reach for it.

She looked gorgeous and shocked, sitting in his bed, the navy sheet drawn up to her breasts, her hair tumbling about her shoulders, her eyes heartbreakingly wide.

'But…I don't understand.'

'What is there to understand?' Each word was bitten off with impatience. Innocent she might might have been, but surely she could figure out what was going on. 'We had a one-night stand. It's over.' He paused. 'If I'd known you were a virgin, I would have done things a bit differently. But as it was…' He shrugged. 'You seemed happy enough with how things happened.'

She blinked as if she'd been slapped, and then she lifted his chin, showing a sweet courage that made his emotions go into even more of a tailspin.

'I *was*,' she agreed with emphasis. 'I may be innocent, but even I can tell when an exit strategy needs some work. And yours sucks.'

'Thanks for the tip, but the sentiment remains the same.' Rafael folded his arms, a muscle pulsing in his jaw. Too many emotions had been accessed tonight, too many raw nerves twanging painfully. He couldn't take any more. She had to *go*.

Allegra took a deep breath, lifting her chin, blinking back tears. 'Will you give me a moment of privacy to dress?' she asked with stiff dignity, and although he could have retorted

that he'd already seen her naked, Rafael didn't
have it in him to be that cruel. Her fragile courage touched him in a way he didn't like, and he
gave a terse nod before stalking from the room.

He needed a drink, something far stronger
than champagne. This didn't feel at all like he'd
expected it to, needed it to. He'd been looking
for satisfaction, and instead he felt more restless
than ever. Restless and remembering.

*'All you have is your honour, Rafael. That's
all that's ever left. Your honour and your re-
sponsibilities as a man.'*

But he had neither now.

The door to the bedroom opened just as Rafael poured himself a generous measure of
whisky. He forced himself not to turn as he
heard Allegra's heels click across the marble
floor of the living area. Remained with his back
to her as she pressed the button for the lift and
the doors pinged open.

'Goodbye,' she said, her voice soft and sad
and proud all at once, and then she was gone.

Alone in his penthouse suite, Rafael raised
the glass of whisky to his lips. He stared out at
the unending night and then, instead of drinking, he threw the tumbler against the wall,
where it shattered.

# CHAPTER THREE

ALLEGRA SAT DOWN in the lawyer's office, her stomach seething with bitter memory as well as nerves. It was the day after her father's funeral, and also of the biggest mistake of her life. She'd left Rafael's hotel suite with her chin held high but her self-esteem, her whole self in tatters, everything in her reeling from his treatment of her.

He'd been so tender, and she'd felt so treasured. Had it all been a lie? *Again?* It seemed she did have to learn that lesson twice. People weren't what they seemed. They said and did what they liked to get what they wanted and then they walked away.

And she was the one left, alone and hurting.

Except, she'd told herself last night, staring gritty-eyed at the ceiling of her bedroom in the modest *pensione*, she didn't have to be hurt by this. Before it had begun she'd told herself she wouldn't be. What they'd done together might have seemed meaningful at the time, but he was still a stranger. A sexy, selfish, unfeeling stranger. It wasn't as if she'd loved him. She hadn't even known him.

She'd made a mistake, she told herself as she rose from bed that morning, body and heart aching with fatigue. A sad, sorry mistake, because she'd given a part of herself to someone who hadn't deserved it. She'd searched for comfort and affection from someone who had neither wanted nor offered neither. She'd survive, though. She had before.

She'd lost her father when she'd felt most vulnerable, had watched him walk away from her without a backward glance. She'd seen her mother withdraw into bitterness and desperation, and she'd fended for herself since she was eighteen. Over the years she'd lost plenty of dreams, and this didn't have to hurt nearly as much. She wouldn't let it.

Signor Fratelli had been insistent that she attend the meeting, although Allegra didn't know why. She doubted her father had left her or her mother anything; if he hadn't given her anything in life, why would he in death? She wasn't looking forward to the meeting, to sitting in a stuffy room with her father's second wife and stepdaughter, the family he'd chosen. Still, it would be a few minutes of discomfort and tension, and then she could return to New York. Act as if none of this had ever happened.

'Signorina Mancini.' The lawyer greeted her with a tense smile as Allegra was ushered into the stately room with its wood-panelled walls and leather club chairs. 'Thank you for coming.'

'It's Signorina Wells, actually,' Allegra said quietly. Her mother had reverted to her maiden name, as had Allegra, after the divorce. She glanced at Caterina Mancini, whose icy hauteur didn't thaw in the least as her arctic-blue eyes narrowed. Her gaze flicked away from Allegra and she didn't offer a greeting.

Next to her, her daughter Amalia, around the same age as Allegra, shifted uncomfortably, giving Allegra a quick, unhappy smile before looking away. Allegra felt too tired and on edge to return it. The other woman had her mother's cool blonde looks without the icy demeanour. In different circumstances, another life, Allegra might have considered getting to know her. Now she could barely summon the emotional energy to sit next to the two women who had taken her and her mother's places in her father's life.

Signor Fratelli began making some introductory remarks; through a haze of tiredness Allegra tried to focus on what he was saying.

'I am afraid, in recent weeks, there has been

some change to Signor Mancini's financial situation.'

Caterina's gaze swung to pin the lawyer. 'What kind of change?' she demanded.

'Another corporation now has controlling shares in Mancini Technologies.'

Caterina gasped, but the words meant little to Allegra. She still didn't know why the lawyer had insisted she be there for such news.

'What do you mean, controlling shares?' Caterina asked, her voice high and shrill.

'Signor Vitali of V Property has secured controlling shares,' the lawyer explained. 'Only recently, but he is now essentially the CEO of Signor Mancini's company. And he will be here shortly to explain his intentions regarding its future.'

Allegra sat back and closed her eyes as Caterina's ranting went on. What did she care that some stranger now owned her father's company? None of this was relevant to her. She shouldn't have come. Not to the lawyer's, and not even to Italy.

'Ah, here he is,' Signor Fratelli said, and then the door to his office opened and Rafael appeared like a dark angel from her worst dreams.

Allegra stared at him in shock, too stunned to react other than to gape. He looked remote and professional and very intimidating in a navy blue suit, his eyes narrowed, his mouth a hard line. His cool gaze flicked to Allegra and then away again without revealing any emotion at all. Allegra shrank back into her chair, her mind spinning, her body already remembering the sweet feel of his hands… *What was he doing here?*

Signor Fratelli stood. 'Welcome, Signor Vitali.'

Maybe because she was so tired and over-whelmed, it took Allegra a few stunned seconds to realise what it all meant. Rafael was Signor Vitali of V Property. *He* owned her father's company. Had he known who she was last night? Was it some awful coincidence, or had *she* been part of his takeover? She pressed her hand to her mouth and took several deep, steadying breaths. The last thing she wanted to do was throw up all over Rafael Vitali's highly polished shoes.

She was so busy trying to keep down her breakfast that she missed the flurry of conversation that swirled around her. Distantly she registered Caterina's outraged exclamations, Rafael's bored look. Signor Fratelli was looking increasingly unhappy.

Allegra straightened in her chair, her hands gripping the armrests as she struggled to keep up with what was being said.

'You can't do this,' Caterina protested, her

face pale with blotches of angry colour visible on each over-sculpted cheekbone.

'I can and I have,' Rafael returned in a drawl. 'Mancini Technologies will be dissolved immediately.'

Allegra stayed silent as Rafael outlined his plan to strip her father's company of its apparently meagre assets. Then Signor Fratelli chimed in with more devastating news—nearly all of her father's assets, including the estate in Abruzzi, had been tied up with the company. The result, Allegra realised, was that her father had died virtually bankrupt.

'You killed him,' Caterina spat at Rafael. 'Do you know that? He died of a heart attack. It must have been the shock. *You killed him.*'

Rafael's expression did not change as he answered coldly, 'Then I am not the only one with blood on my hands.'

'What is that supposed to mean?' Caterina demanded, and Rafael didn't answer.

Numb and still reeling from it all, Allegra turned to Signor Fratelli. 'May I go?' She didn't think she could stand to be in the same room as Rafael much longer. He'd used her. More and more she was sure he'd known who she was, and had planned it. Had it amused him, to have the daughter of the man he'd ruined fall into his hands, melt like butter?

'There is something for you, *Signorina*,' the lawyer told her with a sad smile. 'Signor Mancini had a specific bequest for you.'

'He did?' Surprise rippled through her along with a fragile, bruised happiness, even in the midst of her shock and grief. Signor Fratelli withdrew a velvet pouch from his desk drawer and handed it to Allegra.

Caterina craned her neck and Rafael and Amalia both looked on as Allegra clasped the pouch. She didn't want to open it in front of them all, but it was clear everyone expected it. Caterina was bristling with outrage, seeming as if she wanted to snatch the precious bag from Allegra's hands.

Taking a deep breath, she opened the pouch and withdrew a stunning necklace of pearls, with a heart-shaped diamond-encrusted sapphire at its centre. She knew the piece; it had belonged to her father's mother, and her mother had loved to wear it. Tears pricked her eyes and she blinked them back. The value of the piece was not in its jewels but in the sheer, overwhelming fact that her father had remembered her. She clenched the necklace in her fist, gulping down the emotion, before she managed to give Signor Fratelli a quick nod.

'*Grazie,*' she whispered, the Italian springing naturally to her lips.

'There is a letter as well,' Signor Fratelli said.

'A letter?' Allegra took the envelope from the lawyer with burgeoning hope. Perhaps now she would finally understand her father's actions. His abandonment. 'Thank you.' The letter she refused to open here. She rose from her seat, making for the door.

As she brushed past Rafael she inhaled the saffron scent of his cologne and her stomach cramped as memories assailed her.

His hands touching her so tenderly. His body moving inside hers in what had been an act more intimate than anything Allegra had ever experienced or imagined. She'd understood all along that it had been a one-night stand; she'd known that they weren't building a relationship. And yet the reality had been both harsher and more intense than she'd ever expected—both the import of what she'd shared with Rafael and the cruelty of him kicking her out the door.

Now, on shaking legs, with her head held high, she walked past him and out the door. She'd just started down the steps when the door opened behind her and Rafael called her name.

Allegra hesitated for no more than a second before she kept walking.

'Allegra.' He strode easily to catch her, touching her lightly on the arm. Even the brush of his fingers on her wrist had her whole body tensing and yearning. Remembering. She shook him off.

'We have nothing to say to each other.'

'Actually, we do.' His voice was low and authoritative, commanding her to stop. She paused, half turning towards him, wanting to ignore how devastatingly attractive he looked even now.

'What,' she demanded in a shaking voice, 'could you possibly have to say to me now? You got your revenge.'

'Revenge?' His mouth firmed into a hard line. 'You mean justice.'

'Did you know I was his daughter last night?' Allegra demanded shakily. 'Did it…did it *amuse* you, having me fall all over you when you knew you were ruining him?'

'I didn't know you were Mancini's daughter, and if I had, I wouldn't have touched you. I want nothing to do with any Mancini, ever.' He spoke with a cold flatness that made Allegra recoil.

'Why? What had my father ever done to you?'

'That is irrelevant now.'

'Fine.' She wouldn't let herself care. She intended to forget Rafael Vitali ever existed from this moment on. 'Then we have nothing to say to each other.'

'On the contrary.' Once more Rafael stayed her with his hand. 'We didn't use birth control.'

Five simple words that had her stilling in froen shock, dawning horror. She licked her lips, her mind spinning. She was so innocent, had felt so overwhelmed, that the fact they hadn't used birth control hadn't even crossed her mind. She was ashamed by her own obvious naiveté.

'If you are pregnant,' Rafael continued in a low, steady voice, 'then you will have to tell me.' His tone brooked no argument, no protest.

'Why?' Allegra demanded. 'You wanted to have nothing to do with me last night. Why would you want to deal with my child?'

'Our child,' Rafael corrected her swiftly. He handed her a business card, which Allegra took with numb fingers. 'Naturally I hope this will come to nothing. But if it does not, I am a man of honour.' Cold steel entered his voice, making Allegra flinch. 'I take care of what is mine.'

*Come to nothing.*

An appropriate term for the evening they'd shared, and any possibility emerging from it. Allegra longed to rip his business card into shreds, but the gesture seemed childish. She crumpled it in her fist instead.

'Suffice it to say,' she bit out, 'I have no desire ever to speak to you again, about anything.'

'I'm serious, Allegra.'

'So am I,' she choked, and then hurried down the stairs.

Back at the *pensione*, still trembling from her

encounter with Rafael, Allegra finally opened
the letter from her father.

> *Dear Allegra,*
> *Forgive an old man the mistakes he made*
> *out of sorrow and fear. I cared more for*
> *my reputation than for your love, and for*
> *that I will always be sorry.*
>
> *Your mother loved this necklace, but it*
> *belongs to you. Please keep it for yourself,*
> *and do not show it to her.*
>
> *I don't expect you to understand, much*
> *less forgive me.*
> *Your Papa.*

Tears streaked silently down her face as she
read the letter again and again, trying to make
sense of it. He'd loved his reputation more than
her? What did that even mean? The letter hadn't
answered anything, only stirred up more questions.

And yet…he was sorry. He *had* loved her.
But if that was the case, why had he been able
to let her go?

Rafael sat in the lawyer's office, the acid of regret churning in his stomach. In his mind he
could see Allegra's huge, silvery, tear-filled
eyes, and another pang of guilt assailed him.

He'd handled last night badly. He knew that, yet he also knew he couldn't have changed his reaction. Alberto Mancini had killed his father. What he'd done in exchange to Allegra—treating her harshly after a single night together—was negligible in comparison.

As for a possible pregnancy…he would provide for any child of his, absolutely. There was no question about that at all. But he hoped to heaven and back that Allegra was not carrying his baby. And he wished he'd been able to temper his actions last night, at least a little. Or, even better, that the whole night had never happened.

Yet even as the thought flitted through his mind he knew he was a liar. Last night had been incredible, explosive, the most intense sexual encounter of his life. He hadn't used birth control because he'd been so overcome with desire, with basic, blatant need. He'd wanted her last night and seeing her this morning, looking so pale and proud, he'd wanted her all over again, to his own shame.

'Signor Vitali? Is there anything left to say?'

Rafael blinked the lawyer back into focus, along with Mancini's widow and stepdaughter. He'd thought he'd enjoy seeing Caterina Mancini brought low but, despite the obvious fact that she was a gold-digger, he felt sorry for her.

She'd had nothing to do with his father's downfall, and right now his eye-for-an-eye justice tasted bitter.

And if she was right, and Mancini had died of a heart attack, of shock at having his business bought out from under him...

Then he'd killed Mancini just as Mancini had killed his father.

Uncertainty and guilt cramped his stomach. He didn't like either emotion, would not entertain them for a moment. If his actions had brought about Mancini's death, then so be it. Justice had finally, fully been served. He had to believe that.

Allegra travelled back to New York in a daze, sleeping nearly the entire flight, wanting only escape from the grief and memory and pain.

The world felt as if it had righted itself a little bit when she was back in her studio apartment in the East Village, enjoying the quiet, peaceful solitude of her own space, the sound of muted traffic barely audible from the sixth floor. She'd said hello to Anton, her boss and landlord, and then retreated upstairs. All she needed now was some music to help to soothe and restore her.

Allegra automatically reached for her favourite Shostakovich before her hand stilled, her stomach souring. Had Rafael ruined her favourite music for her for ever? Maybe. She chose some Elgar instead, and then curled up on her sofa, hugging a pillow to her chest, trying not to give in to tears.

A few minutes later her mobile rang, and Allegra's heart sank a little to see it was her mother.

'Well?' Jennifer demanded before Allegra had said so much as hello. 'Did you get anything? Did I?'

'It was a lovely funeral service,' Allegra said quietly, and Jennifer merely snorted. Her mother held no love, or even any sentiment, for Alberto Mancini. 'We didn't get anything,' she said after a tiny pause. Although she didn't understand it, she would heed her father's advice not to tell her mother about the sapphire necklace. 'He didn't even have much to give.' She explained about Rafael Vitali and his takeover of Mancini Technologies, striving to keep her voice toneless, betraying none of the emotion still coursing through her at the memory of that one earth-shattering night. She'd forget it. She'd start forgetting it right then. She had to.

'Vitali?' Jennifer said sharply. 'He bought the company?'

'Yes.'

'Not that it has anything to do with us.'

'No,' Allegra agreed dourly. 'Although Caterina Mancini accused him of practically killing…' Even now she could not say Papa. He might have signed the letter as her *papa*, but he hadn't acted or felt like one since she'd been a child. 'Him. Because the heart attack might have been brought on by shock.' The thought that Rafael might have actually killed her father was like a stone inside her.

*And she'd given herself to this man.*

Jennifer was silent for a moment. 'It's over,' she said at last, and that knowledge rested in Allegra's stomach like lead. Yes, it was over. It was all over.

Over the next month Allegra did her best to move on with her life. She worked at the café, she chatted with customers, she walked in the park and tried to enjoy the small pleasures of her life, but after that one earth-shattering night with Rafael, everything felt dull and colourless.

It was foolish to miss him when he'd treated her so brutally, and yet Allegra felt like Sleeping Beauty who had been woken up. She couldn't go back to sleep again. Retreat was not an option, and yet it was the only one she'd ever known.

So she tried to forget about that evening entirely, but a month after she returned from Italy she threw up her breakfast. She passed it off as having had a dodgy takeaway the night before, but when she threw up the next morning, realisation crept in, cold and unwelcome. The third morning she bought a pregnancy test.

She stared down at the two pink lines in shock, realisation coursing through her in an icy wave. It seemed too unfair that on top of having the misfortune to have slept with Rafael Vitali and then been brutally rejected by him, she now was carrying his baby. One night— and now this?

*Her* baby. Her child, living inside her, like a flower, waiting to unfurl. The maternal instinct was so strong it took her breath away. She hadn't expected it, had never even thought about having children, not seriously. After all, she was perennially single, with no one in the picture or even on the horizon.

And yet...*a baby.* Someone to love, someone to make a family with, a proper family. She would never abandon her baby the way her father had abandoned her. She'd never take out her frustration and bitterness on her child the way her mother had on her. She'd be the best mother she knew how to be, already loving this scrap of humanity with a fierceness that surprised and humbled her.

A baby. A new start, a second chance at love, at life, at happiness. Allegra placed one protective hand across her middle and closed her eyes.

# CHAPTER FOUR

*'Caro?'*

The teasing, lilting voice of the woman Rafael had picked up in a bar only irritated him. He glanced across at her, noting the ruthlessly toned limbs, the well-endowed chest, the pouting mouth. None of it appealed to him. He couldn't even remember her name.

'You can go.'

Her lipsticked mouth dropped open in outrage and Rafael turned away, bored and disgusted. He hadn't even touched her, and he didn't want to. His libido had barely stirred once since Allegra had left his bed. He hadn't slept with anyone, had lost interest.

'Rafael…' She reached out her arms, her pout deepening, and impatience bit at him.

'Seriously. Go.' He gestured to the door of his penthouse suite. He was in Paris on business, and as the blonde beauty stalked towards the door, it occurred to Rafael that he was behaving just as he had before, throwing a woman out of his room.

Seemed he didn't have a great track record.

But, damn it, he'd expected her to call. A courtesy call, at least, to tell him she wasn't pregnant. Although why he should expect courtesy from her when he'd shown her so little he didn't know.

So she hadn't called. Obviously she wasn't pregnant, and he could move on with his life. He could forget Allegra Wells and the sweet purity of her smile, the tears that had streaked down her porcelain cheeks when she'd listened to that music, the way her body had yielded and curled into his, accepting him wholly in a way he'd never felt before. Complete. *Right.*

Idiot.

It had been a casual sexual encounter, one of many, nothing more. Allegra Wells was out of his life…for good. Which was just how he wanted it, because he was done with the Mancinis. He'd taken the man's business, dismantled the industry that had been built on his father's grave.

Justice had been served, and yet there was no one to share his victory. His mother and father were dead, and he didn't even know where Angelica was. The family he'd sworn to protect and provide for was scattered, destroyed. And

Rafael still felt restless, vaguely guilty and un-fulfilled, as if he was missing something...or someone.

'This might be a little cold.'

Allegra winced slightly at the feel of the cold gel on her tummy and then the insistent prod-ding of the ultrasound wand. It was her eigh-teen-week scan, and she couldn't wait to see her baby. She craned her neck to gaze in anx-ious curiosity at the black and white screen and the fuzzy image that suddenly appeared, along with the whooshing, galloping noise of her ba-by's heart.

Excitement leaped inside her as the figure gained definition and clarity—head, arms, legs, beating heart. Everything tucked up like a pres-ent waiting for her. Allegra let out a choked cry, smiling through her tears.

It hadn't been an easy pregnancy. It was over three months since she'd made the decision to keep this baby, three months of debilitating morning sickness, throwing up nearly every morning and twice having to go to hospital to be treated for dehydration. She'd lost weight, struggled to work, and wondered how on earth she was going to manage as a single mother.

Because she intended to do this alone. She couldn't face telling Rafael about their baby.

She couldn't face her child having a father like she'd had, one who would walk away when he felt like it. She still didn't understand what her father's note had meant, and she hadn't dared yet to ask her mother about it, but she'd experienced enough of Rafael Vitali to know she couldn't trust him to stick around.

Still she didn't know how she was going to manage, in a studio apartment with a low-paying job. She hadn't figured it out yet, but she would. Eventually. Now, however, her all of her fears fell away at the beautiful sight of her baby. *Her baby.*

The technician frowned and poked harder with the wand. Allegra winced. Then, more alarmingly, the technician put the instrument down and rose from her seat by the examining table where Allegra was lying.

'I'll be right back,' she murmured, and then left the room.

Allegra lay there, shivering from the cold gel, her gently rounded belly damp and exposed. Unease crept icy fingers along her spine. Technicians weren't supposed to leave in the middle of an appointment like that, surely?

She found out moments later when an important-looking doctor in a white lab coat followed the technician back into the room, frowning as she looked at the screen with the beautiful, fuzzy image of Allegra's child.

'What's going on?' Allegra asked, her voice high and strained with anxiety.

'Just a moment please, Miss… Wells.' The doctor glanced briefly at her file before turning her narrowed gaze back on the screen. Something was wrong. Allegra could feel it in her bones, in her frightened, hard-beating heart. Something had gone wrong with this pregnancy. With her baby.

She lay there, everything in her frozen and fearful, as the doctor took the wand and began to prod her belly once more, murmuring to the technician who murmured back, none of it audible to Allegra.

'Please,' she begged. 'Please, tell me what's going on.'

The technician gave her a smile of such sorrowful sympathy that Allegra wished she hadn't asked. Then she handed her a paper towel to wipe off the gel while the doctor continued to study the image on the screen—the image of her baby.

'Dr Stein will speak with you shortly,' the technician murmured.

Moments later Allegra had all the answers she didn't want. The words reverberated emptily through her, making horrible sense and sounding unintelligible, impossible, at the same time. Congenital heart defect were the three words that hurt the most.

'But what does that mean exactly?' she demanded, her voice shaking. She knew there were heart defects that were operable. There were even some that were asymptomatic, hardly worth mentioning. But looking at Dr Stein's compassionate face, she feared her baby didn't have one of those.

'The particular defect we're discussing is life-threatening,' Dr Stein said quietly. 'The baby wouldn't live past a few months of age, if that.' Allegra gaped and she continued, 'We'll order an amniocentesis as soon as possible, to know for sure what we'll dealing with. This may take up to three weeks, I'm afraid. Based on the ultrasound, it could be one of several heart defects, of varying seriousness.'

'But you think it's a more serious one?' Allegra whispered, and Dr Stein gave her an unhappy look.

'I'm afraid that, yes, it's looking like that, but we won't know until we get the results of the amniocentesis. It's difficult to diagnose this kind of condition from only a scan.'

Allegra walked home in a fog, barely aware of the steps that took her up to her sixth-floor studio. Anton poked his head out of his apartment to ask how she was, and Allegra didn't even know what she said. The world felt muted, as if everything was taking place far away, to other people. Nothing mattered. Nothing at all mattered any more.

She lay on her bed, one hand pressed against her middle. Already, she'd barely been coping, stumbling through each day, trying to survive the awful morning sickness that had exhausted her so utterly. She hadn't let herself think too much about the future, and now it looked like there might not be one. How was she going to wait three long weeks to find out?

And through the haze of her grief and fear, one fact kept coming back to torment her. *She should have told Rafael.* No matter how he had treated her, he should know she was pregnant with his child. He should be aware of what was happening.

Still she resisted. She didn't want to give him a chance to reject her all over again, along with their baby. She didn't want to face his accusations and anger, as he no doubt would be furious that she hadn't told him she was pregnant. She especially didn't want to open herself up to hurt.

Since Rome, she'd done her best to push all thoughts of Rafael out of her mind. She'd told herself there was still time to tell him about the baby, if she ended up deciding that was the best thing to do, which she wasn't at all sure it was. She just needed to feel better first, to find her feet. When she felt stronger, she could think about whether she wanted Rafael involved, even if everything in her had shied away from it.

But now? Now everything had sped up and become urgent. She had to make hard decisions, agonising choices. And Rafael deserved to be a part of that process, even if she dreaded talking to him again.

Allegra battled the possibilities in her mind as the date of her amniocentesis came closer. Finally, two days before the scheduled procedure, she took out the crisp white business card Rafael had handed her outside the lawyer's office. With trembling fingers she dialled the mobile number printed starkly on the card.

He answered after two rings. 'Yes?'

'It's Allegra.' Her voice was a thready whisper, and she straightened, determined to be strong. The silence on the end of the line stretched on for several seconds.

'Yes?' Rafael finally said again, his voice tense, guarded.

Allegra took a deep breath. 'I'm calling because something has happened.' Rafael didn't say anything and she forced herself to continue. 'I'm pregnant and—'

'You're pregnant?' His breath hissed sharply between his teeth. 'By *me*?'

'Yes, of course by you—'

'Then why are you telling me now? You must be halfway through your pregnancy.'

'Almost,' Allegra agreed.

'Then why—?'

'Rafael, please, just listen. I'm pregnant and I had an ultrasound and it looks like there is something wrong with the baby. Something serious.' Her voice caught and she dashed at her eyes with her hand. She couldn't break down now. She had to stay strong. The last person to look for comfort from was Rafael.

Rafael remained silent for a few taut seconds. 'What kind of thing are you talking about?' he finally asked.

'A congenital heart defect.' Allegra drew a ragged breath. 'I'm having an amniocentesis in two days' time to determine—'

'In New York?'

'Yes.'

'I'll be there.'

Shock had her mouth dropping open. '*Be* there? But—'

'Of course I'll be there,' Rafael said roughly. 'This is my child. Isn't it?'

'Of course it is.'

'Then I'll be there. I'll call again tomorrow to confirm the details.'

Allegra wasn't sure what she'd been expecting Rafael's response to be, but that wasn't it. As she hung up the phone she battled between trepidation at seeing him again and a treacherous relief that someone was going to walk through this with her. She was used to being alone, preferred it, but she didn't want to be alone in this.

And yet Rafael? She was, Allegra knew, going to have to be careful. With her baby, and with her heart.

Rafael drummed his fingers against the armrest as the limo cut smoothly through Manhattan's midtown traffic, heading towards Allegra's flat in the East Village. The shock and fury he'd felt that she'd hidden her pregnancy from him for so long had been replaced by a far greater fear for the health of their unborn child. He was going to have a *child*. Someone to protect and provide for, cherish and guard with his life. A life he would treasure, if he ever got the chance.

Rafael had never believed in the idea of atonement, and yet he thought of it now. Perhaps the sins of the past could be righted by this future… his child's future. Perhaps he would finally find the peace and satisfaction he craved, through the life of this innocent.

He'd deal with Allegra's wilful deception later; right now they needed to get through the current crisis…whatever happened. He'd let down those who'd depended on him before and he wouldn't do it again. He would not fail his child.

The limo pulled up in front of a tall brick building. Rafael's mouth thinned as he stepped out of the limo and scanned the names by the buzzers. His eyes narrowed as he saw that Allegra was on the sixth floor, and the building had no lift. She was walking up and down six flights of stairs every day? Surely that could not be good for her or their child.

He pressed the buzzer and her voice, sounding tired and wavering, came through the intercom.

'I'll be right down.'

Tense with anxiety, he shoved his hands in the pockets of his trousers and scanned the building again. It looked run-down and dangerous, a drift of takeaway menus littering the front step, the bins outside overflowing. This was no place for the mother of his child to live.

Moments later Allegra appeared in the doorway. As she opened the door, Rafael tried to hide his shock. She looked terrible—her face was pasty and pale, her hair lifeless and dull, and she'd lost far too much weight. The T-shirt and light trousers she wore for a humid summer's day in the city hung on her like rags on a scarecrow.

Rafael stepped forward to take her arm. She recoiled slightly at his touch, but he held her arm anyway. 'You look as if a breath of wind might blow you away.'

'I've been ill.'

'You should have called me earlier.' He could not keep the recrimination from his voice.

'Please, let's not argue. It's taking all my strength to get through this day already.'

Rafael nodded tersely, knowing she was right. Every instinct in him clamoured to demand why she'd hidden the pregnancy from him when he'd been as clear as he could that he'd wanted to know. But now was not the time. Still, he determined grimly, the time would come. He'd make sure of it.

He helped Allegra into the car, noting the way she sank into the seat with a relieved sigh, resting her head against the leather cushions.

'What did you mean, you've been ill?' he asked as the limo pulled away from the kerb.

'Morning sickness,' she murmured. 'I've had it terribly. I've hardly been able to keep anything down.'

*You should have told me.* He bit back the words. 'Isn't there anything the doctors can do? Medication…?'

'I was prescribed something, but it didn't really help. It's started to get a little bit better recently, thank goodness, and my doctors think it might go away soon if...' She bit her lip, her eyes bright with tears.

Rafael could finish that awful sentence. If she continued with this pregnancy, if their baby was healthy. 'We need more information,' he said gruffly, 'before any decisions are made.' But already he'd made a decision. He wasn't leaving her, and she wasn't staying in a walk-up flat in a run-down neighbourhood. Her place, no matter what happened, was with him. He would protect her and their baby. He thought back to that terrible day, outside his father's study door. He'd failed in protecting those he loved that day. He'd been too weak, too slow to act, too naïve. But he would not fail again. The need to protect his ill-gotten family burned within him, brighter and fiercer than anything he'd ever felt before.

Allegra could feel the tension emanating from Rafael, but she didn't have the energy to wonder or worry about it. All her strength was taken up with preparing for what lay ahead.

She'd barely slept last night, too worried by both the procedure and its possible results. She hadn't even had time to think about Rafael and seeing him again.

And yet now that he was here…she inhaled the saffron scent of his aftershave, felt the coiled, restless power of him, just as she had before. It made her ache. It made her remember. Even now she felt a treacherous dart of desire. How stupid, considering their situation, and the way he'd treated her.

They didn't speak all the way to the hospital, but that was okay. Allegra didn't think she could manage chit-chat, and talking about what mattered felt too hard. The limo pulled up to the front of the hospital, and Rafael leapt out before Allegra could so much as reach for the handle.

He opened her door and with one arm around her shepherded her into the building. She wasn't that fragile, but she craved his protectiveness now. It felt strange, when she'd taught herself not to rely on anyone. Now she wanted to. She needed to.

Before long they were in a treatment room, with Allegra lying down on the examining table and Rafael sitting tensely on a chair next to her. A technician prepared her for the ultrasound, and the now-familiar whooshing sound of her baby's heart filled Allegra with both relief and joy.

She glanced across at Rafael, shocked and then touched by the look of tender wonder softening his face. His surprised gaze met hers and he gave her a smile that seemed almost tremulous. Another point of connection, as sweet as any they'd ever shared, and yet… Could she trust it? Dared she think about what happened next, or in the long term?

'Now this won't take long,' the doctor assured her. 'And it shouldn't hurt too much. I've given you a local anaesthetic to numb the area, but you might experience some minor discomfort and cramping.'

Allegra took in the size of the needle and instinctively reached for Rafael's hand. He encased her hand in his larger one, and she squeezed it hard as the needle went in. It didn't hurt, but it still scared her. Everything about this scared her.

In a few moments it was over, and the technician was wiping the gel off Allegra's stomach.

'Are you all right?' Rafael asked in a low voice, and Allegra nodded.

'Yes. I think so.' She felt shaky and a bit tearful, and she had some mild cramps, but nothing she couldn't deal with. She tried to shake his hand off, wanting to be strong, but he kept holding hers.

'You need to rest.'

'You should take the rest of the day off,' the doctor advised. 'Normal activity can be resumed tomorrow.'

Rafael frowned at that, but said nothing. Together they left the treatment room, and it wasn't until they were in the limo and Rafael was telling the address to the driver that Allegra realised he wasn't taking her home.

'Wait—where are we going?' she asked.

'To my hotel near Central Park.' Rafael sat back.

'But I want to go home,' Allegra said. She wanted her bed and her music and the comforts of the familiar.

Rafael glanced at her, his expression unreadable. 'That apartment is completely inappropriate for a woman in your condition.'

'You mean pregnant?' Allegra stared at him, surprised by his high-handedness even as she wondered why she should be. Rafael had been completely in control of every situation she'd seen him in.

'Climbing six sets of stairs to get to your home cannot be good for our baby,' Rafael stated.

'Plenty of women do that and more—'

'Yet you are the one I care about,' Rafael cut her off. 'And frankly you look terrible—tired, pale, drawn. You need proper rest.'

'Thanks very much,' Allegra snapped. Her feminine pride was hurt by his blunt assessment, even though she knew she didn't look good, and hadn't for a while.

'The reason I look tired, Rafael, is because I've had extreme morning sickness, not because I climb some stairs.'

'It can't help.'

'So what are you suggesting? That I move house?'

'Precisely,' Rafael answered in a clipped voice. 'You will live with me in my hotel suite until the results from the amniocentesis return.'

She stared at him in disbelief. She'd wanted someone to lean on, yes, for a little bit. But not someone to take over her life. Yet should she have expected anything else from this man? 'I can't live with you,' she protested. 'I don't want to live with you. I have a job—'

'Managing a café, on your feet all day? Take sick leave.'

'I can't—'

'Then I shall arrange it.'

Allegra simply stared, too shocked by his autocratic statements to frame a suitable reply. She should have expected this, but she'd been so tired and shaky and fearful, she'd just been glad to have someone to lean on for a little while. Now she was starting to wish she'd never called Rafael at all. 'This is ridiculous.'

'Even so.' Rafael was as unmovable as a brick

wall, his expression obdurate. And meanwhile they were speeding towards Central Park, away from her flat, her job, her life.

'You can't just waltz into my life and make all these changes and demands,' Allegra persisted. 'I won't let you.'

Rafael raked a hand through his hair, taking a deep breath and letting it out slowly. Allegra had the strange sense that he was battling a deeper emotion than she understood. 'I realise you do not want me to tell you what to do,' he said evenly. 'But when you put your emotional reaction to that aside, you will surely realise that I am right.'

Allegra let out a huff of disbelieving laughter. 'What I *didn't* realise is how unbelievably arrogant you are.'

Rafael's mouth firmed. 'This isn't about arrogance. I'm not issuing orders simply to show who's in control.'

'Really?'

'I am considering your health, Allegra, as well as that of our child.'

'And if I refuse?' Allegra asked. 'What will you do?'

'Why would you refuse? You want what is best for our baby, do you not? As do I.'

A lump formed in her throat and her eyes

burned. He dared to suggest she didn't care for their child? 'Of course I do.'

'Then surely rest and relaxation in a comfortable place is it? Why overtax and strain yourself when you don't have to? Why climb six sets of stairs when you don't have to?' He held up a hand to stem any protests she might have made. 'I understand that climbing the stairs might have no negative effect on your pregnancy. But what if there is the smallest chance that it did?' He leaned forward, his eyes burning bright. 'If you could turn back time, do things differently...' For a second his voice choked, and Allegra had the distinct feeling he was talking about something else.

'What would you change, Rafael?' she asked quietly. 'What would you do differently?'

He shook his head, the movement abrupt and dismissive. 'It is now that matters. Now you have the chance to make the best choice for your—our—baby.'

Allegra stared at him, both transfixed and uncertain. 'You can't keep me in some bubble. Pregnant women are able to live normally.'

'Two weeks is all I'm asking. Two weeks until we know what we're dealing with, and then we can reassess. Discuss.'

Discuss what was likely to be a life-threatening condition. The unshed tears that burned behind her lids threatened to fall. Suddenly it felt like too much; her resistance had been feeble but it was all she had. She couldn't fight any more, couldn't stay strong and remote as she always tried to.

'Fine.' She sagged against the seat as the limo pulled up in front of one of the city's most luxurious hotels. 'You win.' Relief and triumph flashed in Rafael's amber eyes, and in that moment she wondered just how much she was conceding.

# CHAPTER FIVE

ALLEGRA BLINKED SLEEPILY in the early evening gloom of the hotel suite's master bedroom. She'd fallen into a deep, dreamless sleep almost as soon as her head had touched the soft, feather down pillow, and judging by the twilight settling softly over the city sky she'd been asleep for several hours.

She stretched and then snuggled under the soft duvet, tempted to stay there for ever. When they'd arrived at the hotel suite, Rafael had been graciousness itself, insisting she take the master bedroom, ringing for some juice when she said she was thirsty, and telling her to sleep for as long as she'd liked.

When she'd crawled into the king-sized bed Allegra had realised just how exhausted she really was, and her last thought before she drifted off was that she was, in the end, glad Rafael had insisted she come here. Not that she intended on admitting as much to him.

Now, as she struggled to a sitting position with a wide yawn, she wondered what exactly she was supposed to do here. What *they* were supposed to do. An afternoon was one thing, but did Rafael really expect her to stay here for two weeks, kicking her heels, until the amnio results came back? And what was he going to do while she waited? How were they supposed to get along? Battling deeper unease, Allegra rose from the bed.

She treated herself to a long, lovely soak in the sunken marble tub and then dressed in her summery trousers and top before heading into the main living area of the suite in search of Rafael.

He was sitting at a desk in a study alcove off the sumptuous living room, frowning down at his laptop, but he looked up quickly as she stepped from the doorway of the bedroom.

His gaze scanned her searchingly from her damp hair curling about her face to her bare feet. 'You slept well?'

'Yes, very well. It's been ages.' It was, she'd seen as she'd dressed, nearly seven o'clock at night.

'Are you hungry?' Rafael rose from the desk. 'I ordered a variety of dishes from room service. I hoped something might appeal to you.'

'That's very kind of you.' After months of

barely managing a mouthful, she knew she needed to eat more.

'Come into the dining room.'

Allegra followed him into the dining room that adjoined the kitchen, which was just as elegant as every other room in the suite. The place was twenty times the size of her studio, decorated with silks and satins, antiques and exquisite paintings. She felt almost as if she were in a museum—a very comfortable, luxurious museum.

'Wow,' Allegra managed, surprised and touched by the spread of food left in warming dishes on the table. She saw clear broths and simple pasta dishes, fresh fruit and half a dozen different salads. Amazingly, despite the constant nausea she'd been battling for the last few months, she felt a little hungry. 'This looks amazing.'

'Take whatever you like. We can eat out on the terrace.'

'Thank you.' He was being so kind, and yet she was afraid to trust it. Reluctant to start depending on his charity and consideration, when it all could change so suddenly…just as it had before.

Rafael handed her a plate and Allegra took it and began to serve herself from some of the dishes. 'How were you able to book the penthouse suite of this place?' she asked. 'I've heard it's booked months in advance.'

Rafael shrugged one powerful shoulder. 'Considering I own this hotel, it was not a problem.'

He *owned* this hotel? It was one of the city's best. Allegra had known Rafael was wealthy and powerful, but it was brought home to her yet again in that moment—along with the realisation of how he could wield that power, if he so chose. How he already had, taking over her father's business. This was man who was ruthless, brutal in his determination to get what he wanted...whatever that was. She needed to remember that.

Allegra finished filling her plate and then took it outside to the terrace overlooking Central Park. The air was a balmy caress, and the terrace was decorated with potted plants and fairy-lights, making it feel like a little bit of the park had been brought thirty floors up.

'This is lovely,' she said as she sat on a chaise and picked at a few mouthfuls of pasta salad. 'Thank you.'

Rafael sat across from her, his plate balanced on his lap. He was wearing the dark trousers and crisp white shirt he'd worn earlier, the shirt now opened at the collar, revealing the strong column of his throat. Stubble glinted on his jaw

and the whiteness of the shirt was a perfect foil
for his burnished, olive skin. He looked, Allegra acknowledged with a pang, as devastatingly attractive as he had that night in Rome.
As irresistibly desirable…except, of course, she
would resist him. She had to, because the situation was fraught enough, dangerous enough.
She couldn't let herself depend on him any more
than she already was. She certainly couldn't
start to care for him.

'I've arranged for you to take the next two
weeks off work,' Rafael stated as he forked a
mouthful of pasta.

'What? How?'

'I spoke to your employer and landlord,
Anton. He understands.'

Allegra's head was spinning. 'But you… Two
weeks?' She blinked at him. 'But—'

'You have exhausted yourself, whether you
realise it or not. You need a proper rest, both for
your own health and our child's.'

Allegra couldn't deny that, but she still chafed
against his commands. She was used to being
independent. She needed to feel strong. 'That
was not your call to make. This is my life, Rafael.'

'And as I said before, I know you want what
is best for the baby.'

It was a trump card he could play every time,

and there was nothing she could do about it, because he was right. She enjoyed her job, but it had been exhausting and she knew she couldn't keep it up for ever. A rest, even one that was enforced, had some merit, as reluctant as she was to admit it to him.

But a rest here with Rafael? Allegra still couldn't imagine spending the next two weeks with him. There was so much they hadn't discussed...his heartless dismissal of her after their night together, her hiding her pregnancy, even the business his father had had with hers. Her father's death. There was so much tension and latent anger and uncertainty—and now they were meant to get along?

And beyond that, she didn't even *know* Rafael. She'd intentionally tried not to think of him since they'd parted, wanting to forget about him completely. She's resisted doing Internet searches, even though she'd been tempted to know more about him.

And now here they were, sitting across from each other, their baby nestled inside her. Allegra didn't know what to think of any of it, how to respond, how to feel. Part of her was clamouring for retreat, while another part recognised that that was no longer an option, not with a child to think of. A child to love.

In any case, now certainly wasn't the time to

tackle any of those difficult issues. They just needed to get through the next two weeks and see what the results of the amniocentesis were.

They spent the evening, incongruously, sitting next to each other on the sumptuous silk-covered sofa, watching TV on a huge flat screen that had been hidden behind an oil painting. After the first few tense minutes Allegra started to relax, enjoying being able to turn off her brain and watch reality TV fluff. And she enjoyed the feel of Rafael's strong body next to her, his thigh touching hers, his arm stretched along the back of the sofa. She could almost imagine this was normal, that she was normal, with a baby and a husband and a life like so many women wanted and had.

Which was a *very* dangerous way to think.

The next morning Rafael suggested they go to her flat to pick up her things, and they rode in silence down Park Avenue to her little studio. It felt strange to have Rafael in her personal space, his inscrutable gaze flicking over her belongings—her framed concert posters, her few personal photos—even the shelf of well-thumbed cookbooks in the tiny alcove kitchen felt revealing of her somehow.

'I didn't realise you actually played.' He nodded towards the cello on its stand in the corner.

'I don't, not really.' She looked away, not

wanting to talk about her cello playing, or lack of it. She hadn't played since she was eighteen years old.

'Do you wish to bring it to the hotel?'

'No,' she said after a moment, her tone reluctant but firm. 'I won't play it.'

'Are you sure?'

'Yes.'

He stared at her for a moment, his gaze narrowed, as if he was trying to figure out what was going on in her head. Allegra looked away. She couldn't explain her complicated relationship to music, how much it meant to her, how it had provided something she knew instinctively people were meant to provide. She certainly didn't want to go into the reason why she'd stopped playing the cello, the dismal failure she'd been. Thankfully Rafael let the subject drop.

After gathering her clothes, books, and a few personal items, they headed back to the hotel. Allegra knew she couldn't put off something she'd been dreading—calling her mother.

Although they lived in the same city, she and Jennifer rarely saw each other. Her mother had her own life on the Upper East Side, tightly enfolded in a clique of aging socialites and impoverished divorcées, trying to live in the manner she preferred with the help of boyfriends and benefactors, and an endless diatribe of high-strung negativity.

Allegra understood the reason for it, knew her mother had never recovered from her father's divorce and abandonment, his decision to end their marriage so abruptly and cut them off with barely a cent, but it didn't make it any easier to deal with her.

Jennifer hadn't been much interested in Allegra's pregnancy so far, except to remind her repeatedly that single motherhood was no picnic, thereby launching down an endless memory lane trip of her own struggles and regrets until Allegra had tuned her mother out. But the mention of a wealthy father to her grandchild was sure to prick Jennifer's ears up and have her asking all sorts of questions. Questions Allegra didn't feel much up to answering right now.

After she'd unpacked in her room, and with Rafael installed in the study on his laptop, Allegra made the call.

'You're what?' Jennifer asked sharply when Allegra had explained she was staying at the hotel.

'Just for a little while.' Allegra took a deep breath. 'Rafael Vitali is…he's the father of my baby. We…we got together when I was in Italy.'

'Rafael Vitali? This is the son of Marco Vitali?'

Startled, Allegra said, 'I...I suppose so. I don't know. Why? Do you know his father?'

'Your father did business with him a long time ago,' Jennifer said after a pause. 'It didn't work out.'

Unease prickled along Allegra's spine. She thought of Rafael's cold remark. *'I am not the only one with blood on my hands.'*

'What do you mean, it didn't work out?'

'It doesn't matter,' Jennifer dismissed. 'It's in the past. But be careful,' she added in an unusual display of motherly concern. 'Your father didn't trust his, and I...I wouldn't trust him either.'

She didn't trust him. Didn't want to trust him. And yet... 'I trust Rafael to care for his child,' Allegra said, because that, at least, was true.

Out in the living area Rafael looked up from his laptop when she emerged from the bedroom.

'You called your mother?'

'Yes.' Allegra paused, wondering how much she wanted to probe the past. 'She mentioned that your father did business with mine, and that it didn't work out.'

A lightning flash of emotion sliced across Rafael's face, too quickly for her to discern what it was, and then he carefully closed his laptop. 'Yes, that is true. They worked together on a mobile phone technology that would now be considered laughably obsolete, and they fell out over it.'

'Fell out?' Allegra regarded him uneasily, sensing something dark flowing beneath his calm surface, and nervous to dip a toe into it. 'Is that why you decided to take over my father's company? Some kind of revenge for what happened before?'

'Justice,' Rafael corrected swiftly. His face remained bland, but Allegra saw that his eyes were watchful and hard.

'What do you mean, justice? What are you not telling me? And why… why did you make that comment about blood on your hands?'

Rafael's jaw tightened, his eyes like chips of amber. 'Now is not the time to delve into the past.'

'But it's obviously important—'

'What is important is your health and well-being.' He rose from the desk. 'I have booked some spa treatments for you this afternoon to help you relax. They are aimed specifically at pregnant women.'

'Oh…' Allegra blinked, startled all over again. 'Thank you.' She felt as if her head was spinning. One moment Rafael seemed as hard and unyielding as granite, and the next he was all softness and solicitude. Which was the real man? Who did she dare trust…if either?

* * *

Rafael paced the living room of the hotel suite, waiting for Allegra to return from her afternoon of spa treatments. He felt anxious, and he didn't even know why. At least, not *exactly* why. Since Allegra had catapulted back into his life he'd been struggling with a tidal wave of fury that she'd attempted to hide her pregnancy from him, and a stronger surge of both protectiveness and fear to keep both her and their child safe.

The memory of when he'd failed his family, his fists beating on his father's study door, his useless words. And then the aftermath. His mother's wan face, his sister's desperate defiance…their whole family falling to pieces, disintegrating before his eyes. It tormented him, when he allowed himself to think of it. The thought of failing Allegra and their child in a similar way or even at all was appalling. Unacceptable. And he wouldn't let it happen. He would do everything in his power to keep Allegra and their baby safe and well. *Everything…* for her well-being as well as his own.

He knew Allegra had questions about his father. His past. The deception and death that still haunted his nightmares and could ruin things between them. She still loved her father—that much was obvious—even though the man had abandoned her. He couldn't tell her the truth about him, not without jeopardising their own situation and Allegra's barely-there trust in him. The past, he determined, would have to stay buried.

The door to the suite opened and Allegra stepped inside, and the clear purity of her smile, the ivory blush of her skin made something twist hard inside Rafael's gut. He suddenly felt breathless, which was entirely a new feeling and made him feel poleaxed, reeling from the strength of his own reaction. He forced a smile.

'How was it?'

'Wonderful. I feel more relaxed than I have... well, ever.' She let out a little laugh, her grey eyes sparkling like silver. 'I've never even had a massage before. And look at my nails!' She held out her hands to him, her nails painted pale pink, and as a matter of course Rafael caught them up in his, drew her to him.

Allegra came easily, caught up in the moment, and he wasn't even thinking as he bent his head to kiss her, already anticipating the sweet, soft taste of her. Her lips parted soundlessly, her eyes fluttering closed, her golden-red lashes fanning onto her porcelain cheeks.

His lips brushed hers and Allegra let out a little sigh. Rafael pulled her closer and then he felt her stiffen in his arms. Her eyes flew open, filled with confusion. She shook her head and then drew away.

'No, I'm sorry…we can't…'

Of course they couldn't. The last thing they needed was this kind of complication… except he wanted it so badly. Rafael raked a hand through his hair, desire surging through his body. He was shocked by his instantaneous and overwhelming response, his heart thudding.

Allegra was still looking at him in dazed confusion, her pupils dilated with desire even as her mouth twisted with uncertainty.

The time would come, Rafael decided. Maybe not yet, not when everything was so uncertain, when their child's future hung in the balance. But the time would come. It had to.

# CHAPTER SIX

'I HAVE A surprise for you.'

Allegra looked up from the book she was reading with a cautious smile. Rafael stood in the living-room doorway, the slight curve of his mouth softening his harsh features.

It had been a strange and unsettling ten days, living in the hotel with Rafael, finding a new and tentative normalcy. It had taken a little while, but eventually she'd been able to relax into a routine. Rafael had spent most of his time working in the hotel's business centre so Allegra hadn't seen him nearly as much as she'd expected to, which was, to her irritation, both a disappointment and a relief. He was often out in the evenings, although they'd shared a few rather tense meals together, neither of them completely comfortable co-existing in this weird limbo.

Rafael seemed as closed off as ever, his inscrutable manner giving nothing away, although towards her he was all solicitous concern, arranging for private museum tours, taxis and, recalling her shelf of cookbooks in her apartment, baking.

Rafael had insisted she order whatever ingredient or implement she wanted, and with a fully stocked, gourmet kitchen at her disposal Allegra was soon enjoying experimenting with new recipes. Her morning sickness was easing and she was actually starting to enjoy food again.

And then, of course, there was the almost-kiss they'd shared. She'd come back from the spa both buzzing and relaxed, and for a moment, with Rafael's warm gaze on her, it had felt so natural, so easy to fall into his arms. To tilt her head and wait for his kiss, that connection.

The shock she'd felt when his lips had barely brushed hers, the deep desire that had blazed a streak of lightning need straight through her, had thankfully made her take a step back. Getting involved with Rafael that way was far too dangerous. She was already well out of her comfort zone, simply being here with him, seeing him in passing in the hotel suite. She couldn't stand an even deeper intimacy, as much as her body craved it.

'A surprise,' she repeated now, her eyebrows raised. 'What kind of surprise?'

Rafael drew two tickets from the inside

pocket of his suit jacket. 'Box seats to the New York Philharmonic playing Bach's cello suites at the Lincoln Center.'

'Oh!' She stared at him in unabashed delight—those were the kind of tickets that were usually well out of her price range, and she was touched that Rafael had thought to buy them. 'That's wonderful. When?'

'Tomorrow night.'

Allegra's smile faded as she admitted, 'But I don't have anything to wear...' Her maternity clothes consisted of a couple of pairs of loose cotton tops and shorts, and soon her burgeoning belly was going to require more.

'Problem solved. I've arranged for one of the top maternity designers to come here with a selection of evening gowns. You can take your pick.'

'Oh. Wow.' Not for the first time, Allegra was both touched and unsettled by Rafael's thoughtfulness and generosity. At times he seemed a million miles from the cold, hard stranger who had booted her out of his bed. But then at other times...

'Thank you,' she said now. 'For all of it. You're very kind.'

Rafael shrugged. 'I thought it might be nice to have a distraction. And when I saw it was a concert for the cello...'

'You're very thoughtful. And a distraction would be wonderful,' she said, smiling shyly. Rafael nodded and gave her the tiniest of smiles back.

The next morning a glamorous woman dressed all in black arrived with a couple of assistants carrying several plastic-swathed hangers each. While Allegra relaxed with herbal tea and croissants, the assistants laid out all the different evenings gowns—silks and satins, above-the-knee and full-length, in every colour of the rainbow. Allegra had never felt so spoilt for choice, or simply spoiled. She felt positively indulged as she stroked the dresses' soft fabrics and fingered exquisite lace.

'I don't know which to pick,' she admitted, and Amanda, the fashion designer, swooped in.

'With your colouring I'd advise the ice-blue. It will make your eyes pop and do wonderful things for your complexion.'

'Will it?' Allegra asked, bemused that a simple dress could do so much. Of course, the gown in question was far from simple, with its diamanté-encrusted halter-neck top and daring backless design. 'I don't know.' She nibbled her lip. 'It looks a bit…sexy.'

'Why can't a pregnant woman be sexy?'

Amanda countered with a little smile. 'You're blooming and gorgeous. Let people know it.'

Allegra laughed. 'I haven't felt either all pregnancy. I've felt as worn and wrung-out as an old dishrag.'

'You don't look it now,' Amanda said firmly. 'And you won't look it in that dress.'

Persuaded, Allegra tried on the ice-blue gown and was amazed at how different she looked. The dress clung to her fuller breasts and slight swell of her bump before flaring out from her thighs to swirl about her feet. The backless design left the entire creamy expanse of her back bare, right to the swell of her bottom. She blushed to imagine Rafael seeing her in something like this. What if he thought she was trying to impress him? *Was* she? Suddenly her feelings were in a ferment.

'I don't know...' Already she was reaching for the diamanté ties, doubtful as to whether she could carry off something like this. Amanda stayed her hand.

'Trust me, no man could resist you in this dress, and certainly not the father of your child.' Her small, knowing smile made Allegra blush.

Did she want to be irresistible to Rafael? Sex was out of the question, and even kisses would complicate their already ambiguous relationship. The last thing she wanted was to be hurt...

again. And yet…she'd felt worn out and ugly for months. The thought of looking good, *really* good, and having Rafael's eyes widen with surprise and then flare with desire…

She was tempted. She was seriously tempted.

That evening, as Allegra got ready for their night out, she started to doubt the wisdom of picking such a blatantly sexy dress. What if Rafael was put off by it? What if he thought she was throwing herself at him? What if she *was*?

And, really, the whole ensemble, from the diamond chandelier earrings Amanda had insisted she wear to match her father's sapphire necklace to the four-inch silver stiletto heels encasing her feet, felt a little much. Some people wore jeans to the Philharmonic. She didn't need to be quite so OTT.

And yet it was nice to feel beautiful. The silky material slithered over her skin and the diamonds winked at her ears. The heart-shaped sapphire nestled in the hollow of her throat, winking and glinting. Amanda had arranged for a make-up artist and hairstylist to finish her look, her hair held up by diamond-tipped pins, with a few curls cascading down to rest on her shoulders. She'd never, Allegra knew, looked so good.

Even so, she was still battling doubt as she left the safety of the bedroom. Outside the Manhattan skyline glittered, the entire city spread out before them. Rafael turned, his eyes narrowing as he took in the sight of her.

Allegra tried to smile but she felt so nervous and exposed that she wasn't sure she managed it. Rafael looked almost unbearably sexy in a midnight-black tuxedo, the snowy white shirt offsetting his olive skin, his hair brushed back from his forehead, his eyes glittering like polished bronze, everything about him radiating that restless energy that had drawn her to him nearly five months ago.

'Is it too much?' she asked with an uncertain laugh. 'The dress, I mean?' Her hands fluttered at her sides and she lifted her chin, trying for pride. She'd chosen this dress. She'd wear it no matter what Rafael thought...and yet she wished he'd smile or say something. He was practically *scowling*.

'You look...' Rafael stopped, his voice hoarse. Allegra waited, her heart fluttering like a trapped bird in her chest. 'Magnificent.'

A smile unfurled like a flower across her face, and then she was beaming. She couldn't help it. A distant voice in her head was telling her not to be so obvious, not to let Rafael affect her. Why should she care what he thought? Why should she want to please or impress him? She shouldn't. She most certainly shouldn't.

And yet as Rafael grinned back that voice was silenced. Tonight she was a beautiful woman, and he was a handsome man, and they were going to hear the most wonderful music together. Allegra wanted to let herself enjoy it without trying to stay safe or sensible. She wanted to forget that she didn't trust him, wasn't even sure she liked him, and that the future was entirely uncertain. Tonight she wanted to leave all that behind and enter into the magic. And so she would.

Rafael had never seen Allegra look so beautiful. She was more than merely beautiful—she was incandescent, breathtaking. The ice-blue of her gown flowed like cool water over her perfect curves, the faint bump of her belly making a deep, protective urge rise within Rafael like a primal howl of possession. She was *his*. No matter what the results of the amniocentesis were, no matter what the future held. His to protect, to provide for, to possess. *His.*

Then he saw the sapphire pendant at her throat and it slammed into him yet again who her father was, who his was, and all the hard history that lay between them…dark, difficult history Allegra didn't know about, but which marked every moment of Rafael's life. History that reminded him that letting someone into your life, even just a little, was a terrifying responsibility as well as a formidable risk.

A faint frown marred Allegra's brow and Rafael banished the memory, the realisation, the fear. Those were not for tonight, when all he wanted to do was enjoy the evening…and Allegra. He stretched out his hand and she took it, slender fingers sliding between his. She squeezed his hand, and it felt like a promise, an agreement. Tonight was for them, for magic.

Wordlessly he led her downstairs to the waiting limo.

The evening felt expectant, although for what Rafael couldn't say. Despite their near-kiss over a week ago, he didn't actually expect anything physical to happen between them. He didn't want it, not if he forced himself to think rationally. If he let his libido lead the way, he'd peel that slippery dress from her creamy skin and have her in the back of this limo.

Yet far more unsettling than his desire for her was his desire to please her. He'd found himself arranging small treats and pleasures for her all week, simply to see her reaction. He told himself it was part of his duty, his responsibility to take care of her. The feeling inside him, as if his heart was a balloon floating higher and higher, was just a fringe benefit.

In any case, he wasn't going to start *feeling*

things for Allegra Wells. After losing everyone he cared about, he was hardly going to let someone else get under his skin. Into his heart. No matter what happened with their child.

The Lincoln Center was glowing with lights as the limo pulled in front of the concert hall where the Philharmonic was playing. Rafael saw more than one man steal a speculative or even lascivious look at Allegra as she moved through the crowd, a stunning goddess with her red-gold curls tumbling artfully onto her bare, creamy shoulders.

She turned to glance back at him, grey eyes sparkling like silver stars. 'This is amazing, Rafael. Thank you.'

Every time she said his name he felt an arrow of satisfaction pierce him sweetly. He told himself it didn't matter.

They took their seats, Allegra excitedly perusing her programme like a child on her first trip to the circus.

Her enthusiasm made Rafael smile as he leaned forward to ask her, 'Haven't you been to concerts before?'

She wrinkled her nose. 'Oh, dear. Is my newbie status showing?'

'It's charming,' Rafael replied, 'but I would have thought, as a seasoned New Yorker, as well as a music-lover, this would be old hat to you.'

She shook her head, curls bouncing. 'No,
not really. Not at all. I've been to concerts, but
they've been free ones in churches and things
like that. I've never heard the Philharmonic play
live.'

'Never?' He was surprised.

She gave him a laughing look. 'Not everyone's a millionaire.'

Billionaire, actually, but he wasn't going to
debate the point. He sat back in his seat, legs
stretched out in front of him. 'Your father had
plenty of money.' Not that he remotely wanted
to talk about her father.

'My father did,' Allegra agreed quietly,
some of the sparkle gone from her eyes, 'but
we didn't. My mother didn't get anything from
the divorce.'

Rafael frowned. 'She must have had some
financial settlement.'

'Nope, not a penny.' Allegra shrugged. 'I
don't know why.'

'She didn't sue for alimony?' It didn't make
any sense.

'I was only twelve, I didn't ask. And I haven't
asked since then because, to be honest, it just
gets her going. She's always been bitter about
it. All I know is my father managed to arrange
things so we were left with nothing.'

Rafael supposed he shouldn't be shocked; he

knew how heartless Mancini had been. But he
was surprised, on Allegra's behalf. Why did
she still care about him when he'd treated her
so badly? 'So how did you survive?'

'My mother sold some jewellery to start, and
she also had various boyfriends who helped.'
Allegra made a face. 'That sounds awful,
doesn't it? But my mother was used to living
in a certain style, and it still makes her furious
that she can't.'

'And what about you? Does it make you furious?'

Allegra shrugged, her gaze sliding away as
her fingers touched the sapphire nestled at her
throat as if it was a talisman. 'I don't care so
much about things. And I've supported myself
since I was eighteen.'

'Eighteen.' Another surprise. 'Did you go to
university?' He realised that, despite having
spent the last week and a half in her company,
he didn't know that much about her or her life.
Not that he'd actually spent much time with her.
He'd intentionally stayed away, not wanting to
complicate matters. Not wanting to get close.
Now, however, he realised he wanted to know
more about her...even if it unwise.

'No, I didn't.' Allegra pursed her lips, her
gaze shadowed. 'I decided it wasn't for me.'

Rafael felt sure there was something she

wasn't saying, but he had no idea what it was. 'What about you?' she asked. 'Did you go to university?'

'No, I went to work when I was sixteen.' He felt his chest go tight, his jaw hard, just because of the memories. His fist bunched on his thigh and he forced himself to relax. 'We needed the money.'

'Then we have something in common.' Allegra gazed at him in sorrowful compassion, and Rafael knew she was keeping herself from asking about their fathers on purpose. Neither of them wanted to prise open that Pandora's box right now.

'Yes, I suppose we do,' he said, and smiled. She smiled back and he felt the tension in him ease.

Then the lights dimmed, and they both settled back in their seats as the music began. Rafael wasn't that much of a connoisseur of music, but he loved seeing the look of rapt attention on Allegra's face. She was utterly arrested, a pearly sheen in her eyes, her hands clasped to her chest. He'd never seen someone look so thoroughly enthralled, and it touched a place deep inside him, a place he hadn't accessed in a long time. It made him yearn and mourn, just as he had when they'd listened to Shostakovich.

Watching Allegra, he wanted to feel as much as she did. He wanted to let himself.

The concert came to an end, the last notes of music fading away into an aching stillness, and Allegra rose from her seat, dashing the tears from her face with an embarrassed laugh. 'Sorry, music always affects me like that.'

In the space of a second he was catapulted back to that night in Rome when she'd said the same thing. When he'd felt as powerfully as he did now, wanting this woman with an intensity that both thrilled and terrified him.

He'd wiped away her tears then, and she'd let him, and then they'd made love. It had been the most incredible sexual experience of his life, and he could remember every exquisite detail of that evening, of Allegra's response, of the way she'd felt under his hands and mouth.

He watched a rosy blush sweep across Allegra's skin and knew she remembered it all too. They stared at each other for a prolonged moment, eyes wide, hearts beating hard, the moment spinning on and growing in strength. The desire was still there, and more powerful than ever. More dangerous too. Would they act on it as they had before?

Neither of them spoke in the limo on the way back to the hotel. Rafael couldn't keep from imagining himself reaching out one hand to tangle in Allegra's hair, drawing the diamond-tipped pins out one by one and then anchoring his lips to hers. He pictured sliding his hands under her gown, hauling her onto his lap so she was straddling him. With a suppressed groan he shifted on his seat, trying to ease the now persistent ache in his groin. He was torturing himself with these kinds of thoughts.

Allegra was quiet, her face pale, her expression thoughtful as she gazed out at the traffic streaming by in a bright blur of light. He thought she was feeling what he was, but even now he couldn't be sure. She'd drawn away from him once already. Even if she desired him, he knew that she didn't want to.

It was a pertinent reminder that, no matter what, sex would be complicated between them. Fraught and maybe emotional. And he didn't need or want to feel more for this woman than he already did. Then his leg brushed hers and an electric current zinged through his body. He couldn't help but feel.

They rode up the lift in silence, and then he was swiping the key card and they were in their suite, the rooms dim and hushed, as if everything was waiting for this moment.

It would be so easy to take her into his arms. To plunder her mouth. To peel the dress away from her body. All the things he'd been imagining, wanting...

Everything, anything, felt possible. He heard Allegra draw a shuddering breath and knew she felt it, just as he did. Just as much.

'Allegra...' His voice was an ache in the darkness, and he reached out one hand, fingertips brushing her shoulder. Her skin was as soft and silky as he remembered. She shuddered again, a ripple of longing that went through her whole body, and he knew, he *knew* she would yield. And he wanted her to, desperately. So desperately.

Then Allegra's phone pinged with an incoming message and in a split second the mood shattered. She slipped away from him, taking her phone out of her clutch and then frowning as she looked down at the screen. A new, different kind of expectation tightened Rafael's gut.

'What is it?'

She swallowed audibly. 'It's a voicemail from the doctor.'

'He called in the evening? While we were out?' His voice was sharp and tense.

'No, this afternoon. I missed the phone call and the voicemail just came in now.' She slid him a quick, worried glance. 'My phone's old. The messages don't always come in right away.

I should have checked...' He heard the recrimination in her voice, along with the fear.

'What does he say?'

Allegra swiped a few buttons and then listened to the call. Rafael watched her face, noticing the way her lips pursed and her eyes clouded, pale red-gold brows drawing together.

'Allegra...?' he prompted when she ended the call. Everything in him felt coiled tight, ready to snap.

'No real news.' She let out a shuddering breath. 'Just that the results from the amnio are in and he wants to discuss them with us tomorrow morning at ten o'clock.'

'All right.' They stared at each other, the weight of the information pressing down making it hard to breathe. The insistent desire Rafael had been feeling had vanished, leaving only cold trepidation in its wake. 'At least then we'll know.' And then what? What would happen to their child, to *them*?

'Yes.' Allegra tossed her phone and clutch on a chair and wrapped her arms around herself. With her tumbled, fiery curls and her ice-blue gown she looked like a slender, burning flame, and Rafael wanted to wrap her in his arms, not out of desire now but to offer her comfort. The compulsion was so strong it felt like a pain, breaking open a scar deep inside him, a barely healed wound from when he hadn't been able to help. To save anyone.

'I should go to bed,' Allegra said softly. 'It's late.'

'Allegra…' He wanted to say something of what he felt, desperately needed to offer her some comfort—and yet what comfort could he give? Tomorrow would bring whatever news it did, and there was absolutely nothing he could do about it.

A shudder racked her body and it felt like a wound to his heart. He hated seeing her suffer, knowing she was afraid, just as he was. Then she lifted her head, regarding Rafael with tear-damp, pain-filled eyes. 'Goodnight, Rafael,' she whispered, and walked out of the room.

# CHAPTER SEVEN

ALLEGRA COULDN'T GET to sleep. She lay on
her bed, staring gritty-eyed at the ceiling, everything leaden inside her. It had been such a
magical evening, going to the concert with Rafael. All night excitement had been fizzing like
champagne through her blood, bubbles popping
inside her head. The music. The mood. The moment when Rafael had looked so sexy and intent…and then the realisation, cold and hard,
that this was all ephemeral and tomorrow reality would return with a dreadful thud.

She pressed one hand against the soft swell
of her bump. *Oh, baby. Stay strong. Be safe.*
Yet she knew it wasn't in her baby's power to
be healthy. It wasn't in hers either.

Around two in the morning she finally rose
from bed, knowing sleep wasn't going to come.
She was planning to make herself a cup of
herbal tea and then sit out on the terrace, watching the city settle down to sleep, but she stopped

on the threshold of her bedroom door, for Rafael was sitting in the living room, dressed only in a pair of loose, drawstring pyjama bottoms, a tumbler of whisky cradled in his hands.

He looked up at her quick intake of breath, giving her a smile that was both sad and wry. 'You couldn't sleep either?'

'No.' She shook her head. 'I was going to make some tea. I'd ask if you wanted some, but I see you've got something stronger.'

'I need it.' Rafael's voice was hoarse, and pain flashed like lightning across his face.

It surprised her, because although Rafael was doing what he saw as his duty by her, Allegra had assumed, rightly or wrongly, that he didn't really want this child. He'd said as much back in Rome, and he'd refused to talk about the *what if?* scenarios until they knew more. She realised she'd assumed he hadn't really cared, not the way she did, and yet now, looking at the set of his jaw, the slump of his shoulders, she wondered if he shared her fear, her agony. If he longed for their child to live and be strong and healthy as much as she did.

In the kitchen she brewed a cup of chamomile tea and then brought it to the living room, curling up on the opposite side of the sofa from Rafael. He looked unbelievably sexy, stubble shadowing his strong jaw and the perfect, sculpted muscles of his chest on glorious display, a sprinkling of dark hair forming a V down to the low waistband of his pyjamas.

But Allegra wasn't thinking about how handsome he looked. She was realising how sad he seemed, and it made her ache.

'I've felt the baby kick,' she said quietly. Rafael turned to look at her, his mouth dropping open in surprise.

'You have?'

'Just in the last few days. I didn't know what it was at first. It feels like bubbles popping inside me. Little flutters.' She took a deep breath. 'But they've become a bit stronger in the last day or two, almost…almost as if the baby knows. As if he or she is telling me…' She broke off, her chest tight with the force of her feeling, the strength of her emotion.

Rafael leaned closer, his expression intent. 'Telling you what?'

'Telling me that he—or she—wants to live.' She scanned his face, looking for clues to how he felt, what this could mean—for both of them. 'That this baby wants to live, no matter what.'

His expression was both intense and unreadable as he stared at her. 'What exactly do you mean?' he asked in a low voice.

Allegra let out a shuddering breath. 'I mean that no matter what the results are tomorrow, even if we know this baby's life is going to be short and hard, I want to keep him. I want to know this baby, I want to hold him, I want to love him. Or her.' She let out a trembling laugh and brushed at her eyes. 'I seem to be rather emotional lately. It must be the pregnancy hormones.'

'I feel emotional,' Rafael said, his voice hoarse. 'This is hard, Allegra, and it might only get harder, for both of us…if you mean what you say.'

'I do, and I know.' But did she, really? The words were easy to say—sort of—but the actions that might test them in later months would be far harder. *Was* she strong enough? There was only one way to find out. 'What about you?' she asked quietly. 'Do you…do you feel differently? Because I won't hold you to anything, Rafael. You didn't ask for this. You didn't even want a baby…'

'I didn't want you to be pregnant,' Rafael corrected. 'And I imagine you didn't either. We were strangers, Allegra.'

'We still are,' she said softly.

'But this child is real and growing and I want it as much as you do.' He took a deep breath, meeting her gaze directly. 'Do you honestly think I would leave you to cope with this alone?' She was silent for a second, and he drew back, deep hurt scoring his face. 'Is that the kind of man you think I am?'

'I don't know what kind of man you are,' Allegra confessed. She knew she was hurting him with her words but she had to be honest for both of their sakes. 'You left me once before, Rafael. You pushed me away, dismissed me out of hand. I'm scared…' *That you'll do it again.* She couldn't say the words, admit so much.

Rafael's mouth twisted. 'We had a one-night stand, Allegra. I admit my exit lines could have used some work, but you can't judge me by a single conversation.'

'Or lack of conversation.'

'If you are going to carry this baby to term,' Rafael stated, 'then I am staying with you. No matter what.' His tone was flat and determined, unyielding as stone. Allegra didn't know whether she should be heartened or alarmed by the strength of his conviction. Was this simply a matter of responsibility and duty, or the heart?

And what was this going to mean for both of them? For their future? She'd intended on going this alone, because that's how she did everything. She didn't want to invite someone into her life, someone who had the power to hurt her, who had already hurt her once before. And yet she couldn't kick Rafael out either. He was this baby's father. He had a say, a right, just as much as she did.

Allegra stared down into the fragrant depths of her tea, her emotions a tangled web of confusion, of opposite desires to stay strong, safe and alone—and to run straight into Rafael's arms. To seek a comfort there that she didn't even know if he could give.

Inside her their baby kicked, and with a tremulous laugh of surprise she pressed one hand against her belly. Rafael drew a quick breath. 'Did you feel…?'

'Yes.' She looked up, a new shyness coming over her. 'Do you want to…?'

'Yes.' His tone was heartfelt, emboldening her to reach over and take his hand, pressing it over her bump, their fingers interlaced. His palm was warm and strong and she liked the feel of it there. 'Wait,' she whispered, and they both remained still, holding their breaths, *hoping*…

And then it happened. A light kick, right into his palm. Rafael laughed, a sound of total joy. Allegra smiled, feeling tearful again. Everything about this was so *much*… Rafael, their baby, *them*.

Rafael kept his palm on her belly and their baby kicked again, stronger this time. He looked

up at her, his smile now one of fierce pride.
'He's a fighter.'

'It might be a girl.'

'Then she is. I don't care either way, boy or
girl. I just want the baby to be…' He trailed off,
a confused torment creasing his features, and
Allegra squeezed his hand.

'Healthy,' she finished softly. 'I know.' Wasn't
that what all parents said? *I just want the baby
to be healthy.* The words sounded trite when you
felt assured of the outcome. In this moment of
terrible uncertainty they were painfully earnest,
and yet it was the not knowing that drew them
together, that made Allegra feel as connected to
this man, or even more so than she had during
that terrible, wonderful night in Rome.

They remained on the sofa, hands interlaced
on Allegra's bump, as minutes ticked past. Their
baby kicked a few more times and then settled
down, and after a while Allegra fell into a doze,
only to wake when she felt Rafael scoop her
into his arms.

'Sorry,' she mumbled. 'I didn't realise I'd
fallen asleep…'

'You're tired.' His voice was gruff, a thrum in
his chest as Allegra pressed her cheek against
the steady and comforting thud of his heart. She
felt so treasured and small in his arms, in a way
she hadn't felt in years, if ever.

Rafael carried her into her bedroom, depositing her gently down on the bed. Allegra looked up at him, still half-asleep, missing the feel of his strength and warmth all around her, barely aware of what she was doing and yet knowing she needed him now more than ever. And maybe, just maybe, he needed her as well.

'Rafael,' she whispered. 'Stay with me. Please.'

A look of surprise flashed across his face and then Rafael slid into bed next to her. He pulled her into his arms, drawing her back against the solid wall of his chest so their bodies were like spoons in a drawer, fitting perfectly. With a sigh of contentment Allegra settled against him and drifted back to sleep. She didn't know what tomorrow would bring, but tonight she felt safe and happy and hopeful.

Rafael sat in the doctor's office, Allegra looking pale and tired next to him, both of them incredibly tense. Now was the moment of reckoning.

Last night had been one of the most intimate and intense experiences of his life—first feeling their baby kick and then holding Allegra in his arms all night long. The ache of desire at feeling her body so tantalisingly close to his had been overwhelmed by the fierce need to comfort and protect her. She needed him, and he wanted to be needed. Wanted to provide for her what only he could.

But this moment, he acknowledged with painful certainty, was outside his control.

The doctor came into the room, her bland expression giving nothing away. 'Miss Wells, Mr Vitali.' She smiled at them both before sitting down at her desk. 'I have the results of the amniocentesis, and there is good news and bad news.'

Allegra's hand snaked out, searching for his. Her skin was icy cold as Rafael clasped her fingers between his own, trying to imbue her with his warmth, his strength. 'Yes?' he asked, wanting to hear the worst and get it over with. Once they knew they could figure out how to move forward. What to do, even how to feel.

'Your baby does have a heart defect,' the doctor explained gently, her smile seeming kind. 'But it is not as serious as it first looked. We'll need to do some tests, but I believe the condition is operable and there is every chance your child will live a full and healthy life.'

Rafael stared at her in shock, barely taking in the words. He'd been bracing himself for the absolute worst news and now he felt blindsided by this wonderful surprise. Next to him Allegra let out a small, soft sob and brushed at her eyes, clearly overcome.

'What kind of heart defect?' Rafael asked. 'What kind of operation?'

Rafael and Allegra both listened as the doctor explained the situation. Allegra would need to have some tests done in the next week, but if all went well then her pregnancy could continue normally to term. She would be scheduled for a C-section to avoid the traumatic effects of labour and delivery on their baby, and then a few days after birth an operation would be performed to fix their baby's heart. The recovery would take several months but then their baby would, God willing, be healthy and whole.

'Besides the heart defect,' the doctor continued, smiling, 'your baby is perfectly healthy, and everything looks normal. Do you want to know the sex?'

Rafael glanced at Allegra, saw a shy hope lighting her features, making her look radiant. She nodded.

'It's a boy,' the doctor said. 'A healthy baby boy.'

*A boy.* Rafael's mind was reeling with the news.

Instead of the baby most likely doomed to die that they'd both been expecting, the awful outcome that Rafael had been bracing himself for, they could hope to have a healthy child. A baby boy whose condition could be healed, who was going to live and grow and know him. A *son*. He was filled with an incredible, overwhelming joy, almost too great to contain, and then realisation slammed through him, leaving him breathless.

This changed everything.

Allegra walked from the doctor's office in a daze of hope and incredulous relief.

'I can hardly believe it,' she said as they climbed into Rafael's waiting limo. 'Our baby is going to be *healthy*...' Again she was both laughing and blinking back tears, overcome by it all as she had been in the doctor's office.

It had been such an intense twenty-four hours, with the concert last night and then learning they would discover the amnio results today. And then those wonderful moments when Rafael had put his hand on her belly and felt their baby kick. Everything in Allegra had ached at the look on his face, and when he'd held her for the rest of the night she'd felt so safe and secure. She'd never wanted that feeling to end.

Since then she hadn't let herself think about any of it or what it meant, because the doctor's appointment had taken precedence. Now she glanced at Rafael and saw the frown that settled between his brows, noted the hard line of his mouth, and unease rippled through her.

She'd opened a part of herself to Rafael last night, had let him in, let him affect her, let him *matter*. All the things she'd promised herself she wouldn't do. It had felt so right, but now she feared she was going to pay the price for her trust and need. And so she scrambled to erect some barrier, find that much-needed distance. And yet how could she, when their baby was healthy? When every emotion she had was scraped raw?

'Rafael?' she asked cautiously. 'You...you are pleased, aren't you? About the baby?'

'Yes, of course. Pleased and relieved.' He paused, swinging his hard, amber gaze towards her and pinning her with it. 'But you realise, Allegra, how this changes things.'

It was more statement than question, and it made her blood freeze. The look on his face was hard and unrelenting. He looked as he had when he'd ordered her out of his hotel room, and she felt the way she had then, uncertain, vulnerable, confused. 'What...what do you mean?'

Rafael's gaze remained unyielding as he answered. 'Before this news the situation appeared temporary. It had an ending point, sadly.' His gaze flicked away from her to the window where traffic streamed by in a blur of colour and sound. His jaw hardened, his profile reminding her of a Roman statue, perfect and cold. 'Now the situation is ongoing and permanent, and that changes things between us, naturally.'

Allegra swallowed hard. Yes, she understood that. Now they would have a healthy child together, a child who would, God willing, live to adulthood. A child they would somehow have to raise together, because it was obvious Rafael wanted to be involved. And Allegra wanted him to be involved. She knew the searing loss of a father. She wouldn't subject her child, her son, to it, if she didn't have to.

And yet…how was this going to work? What was Rafael saying?

*And what if he walked away from her and her son, just as he had before?*

'Of course,' she said stiffly, 'we'll have to come to some arrangement.' Surely they could, although right now she could not imagine what kind of custody arrangement would actually work. She was in New York and Rafael lived in Sicily. They could hardly pass a baby between continents like some parcel, and she wouldn't want that anyway. Anything else, however, was unthinkable.

'Arrangement?' Rafael swung back to subject her to a cold stare. 'I am not interested in *arrangements.*'

His eyes resembled shards of glittering amber as he kept his gaze on hers. 'I…I don't understand,' Allegra said, although she was afraid she was beginning to. Here was the ruthless man who got what he wanted, who took over a failing company, who kicked a woman to the door. Here was the father of her child.

'I'm not going to be fobbed off with some custody agreement,' Rafael stated. 'I would not wish such a thing on any child, and certainly not mine. I'm not going to be satisfied with weekends or holidays, an evening here or there.'

'I think you're being extreme,' Allegra protested. 'Plenty of children have divorced parents and they grow up well adjusted and happy. We can find a way forward that suits us both…'

Rafael arched an eyebrow. 'Was that your experience?'

She bit her lip, caught by the admission. 'That was different.'

'How?'

'Because we wouldn't be getting divorced. Our child wouldn't know one thing and then have to learn another. There wouldn't be a sense of loss, because it would be how it always was, our son's normal.'

His lip curled. 'My lack of involvement would be normal?'

Allegra looked away. 'Why does it have to be your lack of involvement? Surely we can work something out.'

'How? You live in New York and I live in Sicily. A baby's place is with his mother, I recognise that. So what happens? I get our son when he's two or three? Four? Five?'

'No.' The word was torn from her, trembling and indignant.

Rafael gave a nod of cold satisfaction.

'You wouldn't want that either. You don't want to share our child, and neither do I.'

Realisation crept coldly through her, a seeping mist obscuring rational thought. She understood what he was saying, and yet… 'Then what are you suggesting?' she forced herself to ask.

'I want to be involved in our son's life, Allegra,' Rafael stated. 'Completely involved. You cannot deny me that. You will not.'

Allegra stiffened, hearing an implied threat in the words. 'And if I do?' she dared to ask.

'Do not even think of it.' Rafael's voice was a low thrum of grim intent. 'You do not want to experience the full force of my anger and power.'

'Wow.' She let out a shaky laugh, amazed and horrified at how they'd got to this place. Last night he'd held her so tenderly, she'd been halfway to caring about him. Trusting him. Today he was the merciless stranger who had kicked her out of his bed. There was a lesson to be learned here. She'd thought she'd learned it already, but it seemed she hadn't taken it in, not fully. 'You're bringing out the big guns, aren't you? And I thought I'd felt your *anger and power* once before.'

'Not even close,' Rafael answered coolly. 'Trust me.'

*Never.* The limo had pulled up to the hotel. Allegra gazed at the elegant building overlooking Central Park, and felt as if she were about to enter a prison, one to which Rafael held the keys. She couldn't go inside, not willingly.

'We can discuss the necessary arrangements,' she told Rafael in as dignified a tone as she could manage. 'Of course I want to accommodate you as best as I can. I want our baby to have an involved father as much as you do. A completely involved father. We can work something out, Rafael. I know we can.' A bellboy came forward to open her door. 'But I also want to return to my life,' Allegra said as firmly as she could. 'My apartment, my job. Now that we know things are okay there's no need for me to stay here.' And she could use some distance from Rafael and his autocratic commands, his unsettling presence. She moved to get out of the car and Rafael stayed her with one powerful hand encircling her wrist, the proprietary touch shocking her.

'You don't understand, Allegra,' he informed

her in a lethal tone. 'You're not going back to your apartment or your job or even your life As soon as possible you're coming to Sicily to live with me…as my wife.'

# CHAPTER EIGHT

ALLEGRA STOOD IN the centre of their hotel suite, her whole body trembling. *As his wife?* The words he'd spoken moments ago in the limo reverberated through her. With no choice but to get out of the car and deal with this head on, she'd stalked up to their suite and then turned to face him, every atom of her being radiating outrage. Shock. *Fear.* Rafael, on the other hand, looked cool, calm and completely in control.

It was impossible. *He* was impossible. How could he issue such an outrageous command without batting an eyelid? Even now Rafael was shrugging off his jacket and heading for his laptop, as if it were a normal business day. As if their whole world hadn't shifted on its axis.

'*Rafael.*' Her voice trembled along with her body. 'You can't…*I* can't…'

He didn't even look at her as he answered, 'You can and you will.'

'Just like that?' Her voice rang out. 'You want

me to leave everything and marry you? That was your *proposal*?'

Irritation flickered across his face as he turned to her. 'Don't be melodramatic.'

'Don't be *insane*,' she snapped, well and truly angry now. Anger felt better and stronger than the fear that surged right beneath it. Because even now she was afraid Rafael would win. He was richer, stronger, more powerful. And so far he'd achieved everything he'd wanted. Nothing stood in his way, and yet Allegra clung to her ground. She had to, because the alternative... 'I'm not marrying you.'

Rafael regarded her levelly for a long, tense moment. Then he shrugged and went to sit down on one of the plush sofas. 'Fine, let's talk about it. What are your alternatives, do you suppose?'

On shaky legs Allegra moved over to the sofa opposite him and sat down. 'To stay in New York and live my life.'

He arched an eyebrow. 'Working in a café for most likely little over minimum wage, and living in a studio flat in an insalubrious neighbourhood?'

'It is not insalubrious,' Allegra snapped. 'For heaven's sake, talk about being melodramatic.'

'I am not having my child raised in a near-slum.'

All right, maybe her street wasn't the fanciest

in Manhattan, but it was hardly a slum. 'You're being ridiculous.' In all sorts of ways.

'And I think you're being ridiculous,' Rafael countered coolly. 'What about your job, Allegra? How do you propose to continue working with a newborn baby, one that will have particular and crucial needs at the start, and maybe after that as well?'

'I'll take time off, naturally.' She lifted her chin, determined to remain strong. Defiant. She'd meet every challenge he threw at her.

'And do you get maternity benefits with your job? Proper healthcare coverage?' He sat back against the sofa cushions, the twist of his mouth belying the dangerous emotion she saw sparking in his eyes. Despite his level tone, his reasonable demeanour, she had the feeling that he was angry. Very angry.

He was also right. Her job provided healthcare, but it wasn't the best coverage and she wouldn't get much time off after their son was born, plus she couldn't afford the kind of childcare she knew she'd need. All things she hadn't yet had time to think about, much less sort out. She looked away, silently fuming, saying nothing.

'You clearly haven't thought this through, Allegra. Unless you intended to rely on your mother's scant generosity?'

'No.' The word was squeezed out of her throat. She hadn't thought through all these details, at least not enough, mainly because she'd just been trying to struggle through her pregnancy.

And now, thanks to Rafael, she had to think about them immediately. Allegra took a deep breath, trying to steady her jangling nerves. 'I'll admit there are some difficulties,' she said as calmly as she could. 'But that doesn't mean the only other option is living in Sicily as…as your wife.' A blush swept over her entire body at that thought. *Marriage*. In all the possible scenarios she'd envisioned, that one had never even crossed her mind. Yet Rafael now seemed to think it was a foregone conclusion.

'Then name one option that would be acceptable to us both,' Rafael stated.

'I can't,' Allegra retorted, 'because you're being so unreasonable.'

'*I'm* being unreasonable?' Rafael leaned forward, his tawny eyes glittering. 'What if you are the one who is being unreasonable, Allegra? You seem to think it is your right not to have to make any changes or adjustments to your life circumstances for the sake of your child. Is that reasonable?'

'I didn't say—'

'You want to stay in your tiny apartment, walking up and down six flights every day?'

'Plenty of women—'

'Where would you even keep a stroller? Or a cot? That place is minuscule. There isn't room for a baby, and you know it.'

Her lips trembled and she pressed them together. 'I could get a bigger apartment, then.'

'Can you afford it? Or are you expecting me to pay for it—to fund your freewheeling lifestyle while I take whatever scraps I can? What do you think is going to happen?' Rafael demanded, his voice like the lash of a whip. 'I fly over to New York for occasional visits? I don't get to know my son until he's school age? Impossible. I refuse.' He glared at her, his whole body radiating both determination and rage. 'That is not how I intend to be a father.'

Allegra glared back at him, caught between misery and fury. All right, yes, she saw there were problems with her unthought-out plan. Of course she did. But she hated being railroaded into a huge decision, with Rafael expecting her to acquiesce instantly. *Marriage*…she'd never considered it. Never wanted to be that close to a person, that vulnerable—and why would Rafael?

But of course that wasn't the kind of marriage he was talking about. Even so Allegra couldn't countenance it. Couldn't let Rafael have that much power over her. Because, she knew, it would be power. Already he affected her too much. Made her want too much.

'You're not being fair,' she said quietly. 'I'm only four and a half months pregnant, and I've barely been able to keep a mouthful of food down until this last week. I'm sorry if I haven't worked out every last detail of my plan yet. And anyway,' she added, her voice rising, 'I didn't even know you were going to be involved at all until a few weeks ago.'

'Which begs the question why didn't you tell me,' Rafael returned, clearly unmoved by her words. 'I asked you specifically to tell me if you were pregnant. I told you I wanted to be involved in my child's life. And you chose to ignore me.'

'You also booted me out of your bed,' Allegra returned. 'Is that the kind of man I want in my child's life?'

'Now you have no choice.' Angry colour appeared in slashes on Rafael's high cheekbones. 'And no matter how I treated you on that night, Allegra, you had no right to deny me my child. There is a world of difference between ending a one-night stand rather abruptly and refusing me access to my son.' His jaw was bunched, his mouth a hard line. 'Even you should acknowledge that.'

Allegra stared at him, chilled to the very bone

by the dangerous glitter in his eyes, the harsh, implacable certainty in the set of his features. The man who had treated her so tenderly, who had cradled her last night was gone. Vanished, as if he'd never been, and perhaps he hadn't. Perhaps that Rafael had been no more than an expedient mirage. She knew what it was like for people to change. To show their true colours.

'And yet you want me to marry you,' she stated shakily. She felt sick and dizzy, her skin clammy and cold. All the relief at their son's good health had drained away, leaving a dark-edged terror in its wake. The future loomed, menacing and more and more certain. Rafael would not be dissuaded.

'Marrying me is the sensible option,' Rafael answered. 'The only option. I want to be involved in my son's life, Allegra. Completely involved. He's my heir—'

'Your *heir*? It's not as if you're some king,' she interjected. Rafael's gaze narrowed.

'I am CEO of a multi-billion-euro empire. I intend to pass that on to my son, raise him to follow me into what would become a family business. He is my heir, and he is going to be raised in Sicily by both his parents.'

Staring at him, seeing how utterly implacable he looked, Allegra realised how trapped she really was. Rafael had all the power, all the money. If he wanted to—and at this point she wouldn't put it past him—he could use the force of his influence to take complete custody of their child. She could resist all she wanted or dared, but she'd still lose in the end. Maybe even lose her own child.

She pressed her hands to her temples, a crashing headache beginning its aching pulse. 'I need to think,' she muttered. 'And I need to lie down. I'm tired, and not everything is certain, Rafael. The doctor said I'd have to undergo some tests later this week.'

She rose from the sofa, stumbling slightly, and in one quick, fluid movement, Rafael rose to grasp her arm and steady her.

'Rest is a good idea,' he murmured. 'I'll make you some herbal tea to help settle you. Chamomile is what you like, isn't it?'

She glanced up at him in confused disbelief. Who was this man? 'Don't do this,' she whispered. 'Don't be horrible one moment and kind the next. I don't understand it. I can't take it.' *Not again.* With what felt like superhuman effort she shook off his arm and walked alone to her bedroom, closing the door behind her.

Rafael stared at the closed door and swore under his breath. That had not gone as he'd hoped or wanted. Yet what else could he have done? He wasn't going to negotiate, not about something as important as this. He certainly wasn't going to settle for some custody arrangement. And trying to woo Allegra with false words and oozing sentiment had felt like a waste of time and, well, *wrong*.

When he'd learned their child would be healthy all his protective instincts had risen to a clamour inside him. He needed Allegra and their son with him. He needed to be in control. He needed to make sure nothing went wrong. Things would be different this time. He would be different. But first he had to get her to agree.

Impatient and yet resolute, Rafael stalked to the kitchen and switched on the electric kettle. He'd make her the promised cup of tea, at least, to show he wasn't a complete boor.

But when he tapped on Allegra's door and the quietly opened it, he found she was already fast asleep, her Titian hair spread across the pillow, one hand tucked under her cheek, golden-red lashes feathering her pale cheeks. She looks so vulnerable and lovely it made something in him twist and tighten, and he promised right then that he'd make it up to her, to *them*. They could make this work. They would.

Several hours later Allegra opened the door to her bedroom and appeared, yawning and sleepy.

Rafael turned from where he'd been trying to do work on his laptop and mostly failing.

Now he tried for a neutral expression as he watched her stretch, the thin T-shirt pulling across her breasts. 'Did you sleep well?'

'Yes, surprisingly. I didn't realise quite how tired I was.' She went to the kitchen and returned with a glass of water, her hair tumbling about her face in corkscrew curls, her face now set in serious lines. 'You asked me what my life would look like if I stayed in New York,' she said as she curled up on the sofa opposite him and took a sip of water. 'So now I want to ask you the same thing. What would my—our—life look like if I come with you to Sicily?'

Relief and hope expanded in his chest, made his head light. *She was going to agree.* He kept his expression steady, his voice mild as he answered. 'We would live on my estate in the mountains above Palermo. It is spacious and comfortable, with every luxury to hand. A large garden, a pool, every amusement for a growing little boy.'

Allegra nodded slowly, looking less impressed than Rafael had expected or wanted her to be. 'And what about schooling?' she asked. 'When the time comes? And friends?'

'Of course those as well,' he answered. 'There are plenty of good schools in the area and if we could not find one that was to our satisfaction, I would be willing to consider other options.'

She arched a delicate eyebrow. 'Such as?'

Rafael shrugged, his mind racing. He felt that Allegra was looking for something from him and he didn't know what it was. 'We could relocate, within reason. To Rome or Milan, perhaps. I have offices in both cities.'

'Or New York?'

He hesitated, sensing a test. 'The majority of my business is in Europe,' he said finally. 'A relocation to New York is not out of the question for some time in the future, but not now.'

She nodded, her lips pursed, and Rafael waited. 'What about me?' she finally asked. 'What would my life look like in Sicily, Rafael?'

He hesitated, wanting to say the right thing—but what was it? 'You will need for nothing,' he said with a shrug. 'Clothes, jewels, whatever you like. They're yours.' Her mouth twisted and he realised he'd said the wrong thing. Allegra had not been particularly impressed or even interested in clothes or jewels, as far as he could see. *So what did she want?*

The women he'd dallied with in the past had been only interested in material possessions, a diamond bangle, a funded shopping spree in a designer boutique, but he knew Allegra was different. 'And of course you can make the house

your own. Decorate it as you wish. Garden...'
What else might she want to do? 'Music,' Rafael said at last. 'You can have your own music room. Play as much as you want. Host concerts, even.' He was practically babbling, and was irritated with himself for being so pathetically *eager*. She regarded him quietly, saying nothing, offering no encouragement.

'Why don't you tell me what you want?' Rafael bit out. 'Instead of looking disappointed because I can't read your mind?'

She flinched at his tone and he silently cursed himself. What did she want from him? He could give her everything. Everything but love. Rafael stiffened, appalled at the thought. Was that what Allegra was holding out for? Some ridiculous, romantic fairy-tale? Surely not.

'I don't know what I want, Rafael,' Allegra said quietly. 'This is all so unexpected. I haven't had time to process any of it properly. I'm still reeling from the news about the amnio results.' She let out a weary sigh. 'I know you don't want to, but please give me a little time to catch up.'

'Fine.' He bit the word out, still tense. 'But I do need to return to Palermo as soon as possible.'

'Then maybe you should return and I'll come later,' Allegra countered. 'Why must we rush things? We could at least get to know one another first...'

'With me in Palermo and you here? No.' Rafael shook his head, resolute. She would just find an excuse to stay in New York. The thought, stupidly, hurt. 'I want you where I can see you, Allegra. Where I can protect you and take care of you and our son.' His voice thickened, much to his shame. 'That is important to me.'

Her expression softened as her silvery gaze swept over him. 'You have far more of a protective streak than I ever realised.'

'I do. I don't want to let you or our child down.'

'And you're afraid you will?'

'No.' He rose from his desk, determined to end this conversation. It had all got stupidly emotional, and he hated that. He didn't do emotion. It was for the weak. He'd learned that to his eternal cost with his father, when he'd goaded him with his childish complaints. When he hadn't been able to stop what had happened next. *Enough.* There was nothing to be gained by thinking of that now. 'I will never let that happen, Allegra. At least in that, you can trust me.'

Allegra sat down across from her mother, her expression resigned and set.

'You're *what*?' Jennifer Wells screeched.

'I'm going to Sicily,' Allegra answered. 'With the father of my child.'

'But you don't even know him.'

'I know he'll take care of me and our son.' That was at least one aspect of Rafael's character that she was sure of. It had been three days since Rafael had issued his ultimatum, and Allegra had spent those days thinking long and hard about her future. *Their* future. When the further tests with a neonatal cardiologist had revealed the extent of their son's heart defect, which wasn't as simple as they'd hoped but still within the realm of good news, her choice felt even more limited.

She couldn't do this alone. She'd lived most of her life in determined independence, chosen isolation, *loneliness*, but she couldn't do this by herself, and she didn't even want to. But even more importantly she didn't want Rafael or her son to miss out. She'd been denied her father's presence in her life from the time she was twelve. Could she wilfully deny her son the chance to know his father, and Rafael the chance to know his son?

It would be the height of selfish cruelty to choose self-preservation over her family. Because it *was* a matter of self-preservation. Rafael held a power over her, one she didn't fully understand. She was attracted to him physically, of course, but she'd felt stirrings of something even deeper. When he held her…when he'd felt the baby kick…if she let herself, she could start to care for him, and that would be a disaster. Because there was every chance Rafael would walk away from her as her father had. But he wouldn't, she prayed, walk away from their son.

And so she'd told Rafael she would go to Sicily, but she wouldn't marry him—not yet, anyway. They needed to get to know one another before she made actual vows, agreed to that level of commitment. To her surprise, Rafael had acquiesced. Tersely, but still. She'd been half expecting him to frog-march her down the aisle.

Then yesterday she'd gone to her apartment and packed up what she'd wanted to take, which had been surprisingly little. Looking around the tiny space, she wondered at how she had ever thought she could have managed there with a baby. And yet how she was going to manage in this strange new life in Sicily? So much was unknown.

'I can't believe you're doing this, Allegra.' Jennifer's voice rang out in censure. 'This stranger…running away with him? Have you thought this through at all?'

'Yes, and it makes sense,' Allegra answered. 'Considering the alternatives.' She felt weary right down to her toes, and tomorrow evening they were leaving for Palermo. She'd already handed in her notice for her job, said goodbye to Anton, who had been her friend and boss for nearly ten years. He'd kissed her on both cheeks with tears in his eyes.

'Is Vitali being…difficult?' Jennifer asked after a moment. She looked on edge.

'Pragmatic,' Allegra said, even as she wondered why she was being loyal to Rafael. Perhaps because, in his own hard way, he was being loyal to her. And whether she liked it or not, they were a family now. 'As am I.'

'You remember what I told you about his father?' Jennifer said, and now she sounded diffident.

'He did business with my father and it didn't work out, you said.' But it was more than that. Blood on his hands. What had happened? How much did it matter? She couldn't ask Rafael now; things between them were tense enough.

'Yes, and your father didn't trust him.' Jennifer expelled a breath. 'I don't know the details, of course, but there has to be a reason for that. I got the sense that there might have been something…' She paused, pursing her lips. 'Criminal involved.'

'Criminal?' Allegra stared at her, appalled by this new revelation. 'What do you mean exactly?'

Jennifer shrugged, her gaze siding away. 'I

don't really know, but soon after they did business Vitali went broke. He lost everything, and narrowly avoided prison. That's…that's all I know. Perhaps it's better buried in the past.'

It was more than Allegra had ever known, and underscored how little she knew Rafael or his history. How little he'd told her. She'd have to ask sometime, and while she didn't look forward to that conversation, she needed to know what she was getting into. What their child was getting into. She needed to trust Rafael… yet how could she, when she didn't know him? When she didn't like to trust anyone?

'That might be so,' Allegra told her mother, 'but Rafael has his own business and I really don't think it involves any criminal activities.' At least she hoped not.

'But you can't be sure.'

'No.' She couldn't, Allegra knew with a pang of true fear, be sure about anything.

# CHAPTER NINE

ALLEGRA GAZED OUT the window of the passenger jet at the hard blue sky, not a cloud in sight, and tried to bolster her courage as well as calm her seething nerves. They were due to land in Palermo in less than an hour, and after a sleepless night in the first-class cabin she felt exhausted and overwhelmed.

'Do you need anything?' Rafael asked as he looked up from his tablet where he'd been scanning the morning news. 'Herbal tea? A hot compress?'

'I'm fine.' He'd been all solicitousness for the flight, but it was a formal, distant concern that set Allegra's nerves on edge. She felt like his patient, or perhaps his possession. Maybe both. And she was conscious, more than ever, of how much she'd left behind. Her job. Her life. Freedom and independence.

'How far is your villa from the airport?' she asked, and Rafael put his tablet aside.

'About an hour. A limo will pick us up.'

She nodded, gripping the armrests, wishing she felt more at ease. More confident that she was doing the right thing. She'd be living in the lap of luxury after all. Rafael had promised her just about anything she wanted. And yet…he could be such a hard man. Even when he was being kind there was a distance to him, a remoteness that made her uneasy. And she knew no one in Sicily other than him. Their baby wasn't due for over four months. What would she do all day? Could she be happy?

'Please don't worry,' Rafael murmured, resting one long, lean hand on top of hers. 'It will all be fine.'

Allegra nodded again. Rafael squeezed her hand, and the simple touch had the power to affect her, reminded her that despite all their differences they did have chemistry. Chemistry Rafael no doubt expected them to act on…but when? She couldn't even begin to think about *that*. Sex seemed like an impossibility, although the doctor had, with a smile and a wink, given them the all-clear.

'There's no reason,' he'd said, looking at them both, 'why you can't have a normal pregnancy from now until your delivery…and a normal sex life.'

Allegra had blushed and stared down at her

lap. Rafael had said nothing. She had no idea what to expect from him, from anything, and it made her feel uncertain. Vulnerable. Which was a feeling she hated.

'Please prepare for landing.'

Allegra put her seat up as the steward went through the cabin and the plane began its descent. Below she could see Sicily spread out in a living map: dusty, rocky hills and towns with red-roofed buildings that looked as if they were clinging to the mountainside. It was unfamiliar and yet it struck a chord, reminded her suddenly and sweetly of her childhood in Italy. A soft sigh escaped her and Rafael gave her a sharp look.

'Are you all right?'

'Yes, I was just thinking about when I lived here. That is, in Italy.' She gave him a small smile. 'It feels like a lifetime ago.'

'You lived in Rome?'

'I lived in Rome during the school year,' she answered, 'and spent summers at our estate in Abruzzi. I loved it there.' The land had been harsh and rugged and unrelentingly beautiful, snow-capped mountains piercing a brilliantly blue sky. She'd loved the quiet, the sense of solitude and stillness and peace. It had spoken to her shy, solitary spirit.

'You missed it?' Rafael asked after a moment.

'Yes, especially because my first year in New

York was so awful.' She shook her head at the memory, her mouth twisting.

'What was so awful about it?'

'Everything. My English was terrible, and the school was big and rough—I felt lost. I was teased too, but it helped when I kept myself to myself. Then I was just invisible.'

Rafael frowned. 'That doesn't sound like much fun.'

'No, but I've always liked my own company.' She paused. 'It's easier, isn't it, not to depend on anyone? Not to care.'

Rafael didn't respond, merely frowned and looked out the window. Allegra wondered what he was thinking and decided not to ask. Better not to share any more feelings than she already had.

The plane touched down with a bump, and for the next hour they were kept busy clearing Immigration and collecting their luggage.

By the time Allegra slid into the limo she felt exhausted, and although she'd meant to take in the scenery on the drive to Rafael's estate, she ended up falling asleep as the limo climbed narrow, twisting roads, making the steep ascent into the mountains.

When Rafael nudged her gently awake she discovered she was lying on the seat, her head in his lap, her cheek resting on his powerful thigh. Rafael's hand rested lightly on her hair. It felt wonderful and alarming at the same time, and she scrambled up to a sitting position as quickly as she could. 'Sorry,' she mumbled as she pushed tangled hair away from her eyes. She felt thick-headed, her body clock completely out of synch, and she had a feeling she looked like a disaster. 'I didn't even realise I'd fallen asleep.'

'You were tired. We're here now, and after the doctor checks you out you can have a proper rest.'

Allegra looked at him in confusion. 'The doctor?'

'I've put a doctor on retainer for the duration of your pregnancy. He's living in one of the estate's cottages. It seemed sensible, considering the remoteness of our location. Of course, Palermo's emergency medical facilities are less than an hour away, and I have a helicopter on the estate.'

She stared at him in surprise. 'But the doctor in New York said my pregnancy was normal, Rafael. This seems a bit excessive.' Which was massive understatement. She didn't need a doctor on call, surely. And yet Rafael looked obdurate.

Rafael flicked a glance at her. 'There is no harm in taking precautions. You want what's best for our son, don't you?'

Once again he was playing that trump card.

Allegra decided not to argue. She was too tired, and she supposed there was no reason to mind having a doctor around.

Rafael opened the door to the limo and ushered her out, one hand resting on her elbow as he guided her towards the villa. Allegra paused on the portico, breathing in the warm, fir-scented air as she took in the curving drive that snaked through dense trees, the rolling, rocky hills visible beyond.

She turned to the house, a sprawling and imposing villa of weathered stone, its double doors of ancient, scarred wood now flung open. A smiling, red-cheeked woman, her greying hair piled on top of her head in a round bun, gave them both a wide smile while next to her a tall, lanky man nodded and bowed.

'This is Maria and Salvatore, my housekeeper and groundsman,' Rafael explained to Allegra. He spoke in Italian, which he hadn't done with her all the time they'd been in New York, and even though it was her native language, after so many years in America it took Allegra a moment to make the adjustment.

Maria came forward, exclaiming about her bump, and then kissed her soundly on both cheeks. Salvatore bowed again. The exchange heartened Allegra, and made her feel a little less alone.

'Now is not the time for a tour,' Rafael said.
'Since you are tired. I'll show you your room
and then summon the doctor.'

'I'm fine…' Allegra protested, because now
that she was here she wanted to explore. From
the soaring foyer she could see a comfortable
looking lounge with huge sofas in cream linen
and French doors overlooking a terrace. On the
other side she saw the cheerful yellow walls
of a large kitchen, and another set of French
doors leading to what looked like a large vege-
table garden. All of it made her want to see and
know more. She felt the stirrings of excitement,
which was a welcome change from all the ap-
prehension.

'You need to rest,' Rafael said, clearly brook-
ing no argument, and with his hand on her
elbow he guided her up the curving stairs to a
large bedroom. While he went to fetch the doctor, Allegra explored the room—it was every
bit as luxurious as the one she'd enjoyed in the
hotel back in New York.

There was a huge king-sized bed on its own
dais, a massive fireplace that would make the
room cosy in winter, and wide windows whose
shutters were open to the tumbling garden
below. She rested her elbows on the stone sill
as she took in the infinity pool sparkling under
the sunlight, and the tangle of bougainvillea and

hibiscus that covered the steep hillsides. The air was warm and dusty, scented with rosemary and pine. She felt as if she'd stumbled into paradise.

'The doctor will examine you now.'

Allegra turned to see a stern-looking, white-haired man with an old-fashioned black bag standing in the doorway, and her heart sank. Determined to be as accommodating as possible, she submitted to a battery of routine checks while Rafael watched.

'I really am fine,' she said as the doctor tucked his stethoscope away. 'Everything's fine.'

'Well?' Rafael turned to the doctor for his verdict, and Allegra gritted her teeth. Since when had she become incapable of speaking for herself?

'She's a little dehydrated,' the man said. 'And she needs some rest.'

Rafael nodded. 'Thank you.' He turned to Allegra once the man had thankfully left. 'I'll have Maria bring up some water. You should drink at least two glasses.'

Allegra folded her arms. 'I'm capable of making my own decisions, Rafael.'

His mouth thinned as he arched one dark eyebrow. 'You are fighting me on this small matter?'

'Yes, because you're treating me like an idiot. I don't need to be fussed over by a doctor every moment.'

'I simply wanted you to be checked out after our travel. What is the problem?'

She stared at him, frustrated, because he made it sound so reasonable. It was his attitude she didn't like, the high-handed way he dealt with everything. With her.

'The problem is you're being aggravatingly bossy.'

'I am caring for our child.'

'Which is very important to you, I know. I get that, trust me. But you can't…you can't be in control of everything.'

Rafael bit back a response and then looked away. 'This is important to me, Allegra,' he said after a moment. 'I don't want to fail in my duty as a father. Please…indulge me.'

A bleak look had come into his eyes, and it made her wonder what hidden hurts Rafael was keeping from her. Or was she just being fanciful, and he was simply an arrogant, autocratic, domineering man? From the obdurate look on his face Allegra knew she'd get nowhere pressing the point now.

'Fine, I'll indulge you,' she said wearily. 'At least in this.'

Several hours later she woke from a deep sleep and stretched languorously. Long, golden rays of late afternoon sunshine slid across the floor.

She'd been asleep for hours, so clearly she'd needed the rest.

Allegra got out of bed and went to explore the huge en suite bathroom, enjoying the enormous marble walk-in shower. Dressed in a strappy sundress, her hair damp and curling about her shoulders, she headed downstairs in search of Rafael.

She didn't find him, but she did see Maria in the kitchen, and the housekeeper bustled around to have Allegra sit at the round kitchen table and then plied her with iced tea and fig cookies.

'Something smells delicious,' Allegra said.

'Ah, it is a welcome feast for Signor Vitali and his lovely lady,' Maria said with a smile. 'It has been a long time since I have been able to cook so much!'

'Is it?' Allegra nibbled a cookie, wondering how much she could press the housekeeper for information. 'Has Rafael not had…guests here before?'

Maria gave her a shrewdly knowing look. 'Signor Vitali has never had anyone here before. He has always been a very solitary man. Salvatore and I have served him for more than ten years.' She smiled fondly. 'He worked so hard, he had little time for anything else.' She nodded meaningfully towards Allegra's bump. 'Perhaps now that will change.'

'Perhaps.' Although Rafael had certainly immersed himself in work since he'd come back into her life. Despite his insistence that he wanted to be an involved father, Allegra wondered if he simply wanted to be in control.

Replete with cookies and tea, she wandered out of the kitchen to explore the villa—and find Rafael. She discovered the lounge she'd seen earlier and a media room with a huge flat-screen TV and a state-of-the-art sound system. A dining room with a table that easily seated twelve was empty, as was a smaller room with a cosy table for four. She slipped through the French windows onto the terrace that overlooked the infinity pool, breathing in the scents of bougainvillea and rosemary. The sun was setting, painting the sky with livid violet streaks, and she heard birds chirping in the tall, stately firs that surrounded the villa on most sides, the mountains towering above them.

But where was Rafael—and why did she want to find him so badly? Perhaps he intended for them to live separate lives here in Sicily, a prospect that filled her with a treacherous disappointment. She wanted to know what their future was going to look like…and, she realised, she wanted to know Rafael. It had been all right to maintain a holding pattern while they'd waited for the amnio results, but now they were meant to have some kind of life together. Rafael was insisting they marry, and while that prospect still filled her with fear, it also made her want to get to know the man she might be spending the rest of her life with, at least a little. So where was he?

Maria had started to serve dinner in the smaller dining room, several fragrant dishes that made Allegra's mouth water. Then she noticed the place setting for one.

'Is Rafael not eating?' she asked, hating how small her voice sounded.

Maria made a face. 'Signor Vitali said he needed to work tonight.'

So the feast was for her alone. Allegra sat at the table and nibbled course after delicious course, feeling sorry both for herself and for Maria, who had gone to so much effort for her employer. Why had Rafael refused to come down for dinner? Surely his work couldn't be that important. Was he avoiding her on purpose, setting the pattern for their married lives?

Loneliness swamped her at the thought. Already she was losing that sense of independence she'd maintained for so long. She wanted Rafael with her, needed his presence in a way that made her feel unsettled. She wasn't used to needing people. Depending on them. Perhaps it was better this way…except it didn't *feel* better.

At the end of the meal she took her decaf coffee out onto the terrace, curling up on a lounger as she watched the stars appear in the sky, like diamond pinpricks in a bolt of black velvet. He was avoiding her, she acknowledged with leaden certainty. He had to be. To absent himself all afternoon and then through the evening… He was telling her how he intended things to be, and Allegra didn't like it. If he was going to leave her alone, she might as well have stayed in New York.

She liked it even less when she woke up the next morning to an empty-feeling house. Maria was in town at the market and Salvatore was outside, working in the garden. Rafael was nowhere to be found.

She decided to go for a walk—only to be told, regretfully, by Salvatore that Signor Vitali had forbidden her from leaving the formal gardens, as the mountainside was steep and dangerous. Allegra looked at the high stone walls, the whole world shimmering out of reach, and realised she was truly trapped.

She stalked inside the villa, fury rising in her like a tidal wave. So she'd been brought to this beautiful estate to be kept as a prisoner. She didn't know what hurt most—Rafael's controlling attitude or his deliberate absence. She stewed for most of the morning while Rafael kept his distance, and then finally she'd had enough. She'd find him, and, by heaven, she'd tell him what was on her mind.

'Where is Signor Vitali?' she asked Salvatore, who looked shocked by her strident tone.

'He is working...'

'Where?'

'In his study, but he does not wish to be disturbed.'

'Perhaps he needs to be disturbed,' Allegra answered. 'Could you please tell me where his study is?'

'I don't think—'

'Tell her, Salvatore,' Maria said quietly, coming into the room behind Allegra. 'She is carrying his child. She deserves to talk to him. And Signor Vitali...he needs company too.'

With a shrug of his thin shoulders Salvatore pointed upstairs. 'The top floor. A room on its own.'

Allegra stalked upstairs, her anger giving her a boldness she hadn't known she'd possessed. A narrow, twisting staircase at the end of the corridor led to a single room on the villa's top floor, its heavy, oak door shut fast. She knocked on the door hard enough to bruise her knuckles.

After a pause she heard Rafael's gruff voice. 'Salvatore?'

'No. Allegra.' She turned the handle, gratified when it opened, and walked into the room.

Rafael's study was spacious, with wide windows on three sides offering stunning views of the mountains. A huge mahogany desk took up the centre of the room, and Rafael sat at it, his eyes narrowed, his mouth compressed.

Allegra planted her hands on her hips as she faced him. 'If I'd known you were going to imprison me here, I wouldn't have agreed to come.'

'Imprison?' Rafael arched one eyebrow. 'I'd hardly call this a prison.'

'I'm serious, Rafael. Since we've arrived you haven't shown your face once—'

'I have much work to catch up on.'

Allegra hesitated for a second, wondering if she was overreacting. Wondering why she wanted his company so much, why she felt so *hurt*. Then she took a deep breath and ploughed on. 'So why can't I even take a walk?'

Rafael's nostrils flared. 'These are simply measures to ensure your safety.'

'I'm not made of glass,' Allegra burst out. 'I'm not going to *break*.'

For a second Rafael's face contorted, and then he looked away. 'You don't know that,' he said quietly. 'Anything could happen, Allegra.' His voice went hoarse. 'Anything.'

Allegra stared at him in confusion, her heart twisting at the look of bleak despair on his face. 'Rafael...' she asked softly. 'What is it that you're so afraid of?'

'I'm not...' he let out a shuddering breath, wiping his hand over his face '...losing you. Losing our child.' He turned away, dropping his hand, the set of his shoulders resolute once more, that brief glimpse of raw vulnerability gone. 'We came close to losing this baby, Allegra, or at least thinking we were going to lose it. Him. I don't ever want to feel that again.'

She stared at him, wishing she understood more. Wishing she knew how to reach him. 'You can't control everything, you know,' she said quietly. 'You can't prevent accidents from happening, or just life. I need to live, Rafael—'

'You are living,' he cut her off dismissively. 'Enjoy the villa and all it has to offer. Lounge by the pool.'

'I don't want to spend every day *lounging*.'

His expression closed up. 'I really do not know what you are complaining about.' And with that he angled his body away from her, pulling a sheaf of papers towards him. So she was being dismissed, like some unruly servant. He wouldn't even look at her any more. This was how Rafael dealt with people. He wasn't overprotective, he was compulsively controlling. And it hurt to realise she was just a cog to him, something to move and manipulate accordingly. Stupidly it hurt, because she hadn't wanted to let herself care. Yet here she was, caring. Hurting.

She stood there for a moment, watching him work, seeing the way he'd completely blanked her out. It was as if she no longer existed. His gaze didn't flick to her once.

She felt the fury rise again, but with it something far worse. Despair. She couldn't fight this. Arguing with Rafael, just trying to have a reasonable discussion with him, was like battering her head—her heart—against a brick wall. Because now that she was here, now that she'd come into his life and brought him into hers, she wanted more than this. And she had no idea how to get it.

Without a word she turned on a heel and left his study, slamming the door behind her. The loud thwack as it crashed against the doorframe was satisfying even though she knew the gesture was pointless and childish.

She walked downstairs, fury still pounding through her, along with the despair. She wrenched open the French doors to the terraced gardens, causing Maria to bustle in from the kitchen, her expression alarmed.

'*Signorina*—'

'I'm just going for a walk.'

Maria frowned. 'Signor Vitali—'

'I don't care about Signor Vitali.' Allegra cut her off, wishing it were true, and she walked out of the house.

# CHAPTER TEN

FROM THE WINDOW of his study Rafael watched Allegra stride through the gardens, her entire body rigid with affront. He fought the urge to run after her, insist she return to the villa. Keep her safe. He couldn't control everything, but he'd damned well try. The alternative was unthinkable.

His gaze narrowed as he saw Allegra make her way through the garden to the latticed gate in the high stone wall. He'd forbidden her from leaving the formal gardens, didn't want her to navigate the steep and rugged mountain terrain surrounding the estate. Cursing under his breath, he saw Allegra wrench open the gate and then stride through the forest, swallowed up by the trees and the dark.

He waited an hour before he went out looking for her, just to show how reasonable he could be. A tense, endless hour when his mind raced with worst-case scenarios and he did his best to stave off the panic he felt skirting the edges of his mind, blurring rational thought. Memories danced like shadows in his mind, of his mother, his sister, his father. Their faces, their words, closed doors, shattered hope.

With a muttered curse Rafael flung open the door to his study. He yanked on a pair of hiking boots and headed outside, the air hot and dusty and dry, the sun beating hard on his head. She shouldn't have been out in this heat. He didn't even know if she'd put on sunscreen. And what about a sunhat and proper walking shoes? What if she'd tripped or fallen? His stomach clenched hard and he tasted the metallic tang of fear as he followed her path through the gate, picking up her trail through the broken ferns and grasses along the mountainside. With each step his anxiety grew and his fists clenched at his sides. He felt deep in his gut that something was wrong, that something had happened on his watch. *Again.*

For a second he could see his mother's empty eyes, his sister's wasting body. His *father…*

Dammit, he couldn't keep opening the door to all that remembered pain. What was it about Allegra that brought it to the surface? He needed to lock that door tightly, so tightly, before the memories surged around him and he drowned.

He'd been walking for about fifteen minutes, calling Allegra's name, his voice starting to grow hoarse with panic, when he saw her. She was crumpled up at the bottom of a large boulder, one leg awkwardly angled beneath her, her head lolling back. Her eyes were closed but they fluttered open as Rafael ran towards her, cradling her head in his lap as he said her name over and over again, tears of grief and self-recrimination springing to his eyes.

Her eyes fluttered open and fastened on his. 'Next you're going to handcuff me to my bed,' she murmured. Her face was pale and waxy with a pearly sheen of perspiration but her tiny smile made Rafael's heart turn over. 'Just spare me the I-told-you-so, please.'

'Are you hurt?' Rafael demanded, his hands shaking as he ran them lightly over his body, looking for bruises or broken bones.

'My ankle,' Allegra answered on a shuddery sigh. 'It's not broken. At least, I don't think it is. But I tripped on that stupid rock and went sprawling.' She pressed one hand to her bump, her voice trembling and her face crumpling as she added, 'I think the baby's all right.'

Rafael's insides felt icy as he bundled her in his arms. She felt light and precious, a treasure he wanted to cling to for ever. *The mother of his child.* 'Let's get you home,' he said, and, scooping her up, he started back towards the villa.

* * *

The trip back to the villa was a blur; Allegra curled into Rafael, resting her cheek against the hard wall of his chest, taking comfort from the steady thud of his heart. The last hour she'd spent trapped in the woods, the trees dark and menacing all around her, her ankle throbbing, had been truly awful. She'd been afraid for their baby, afraid for herself, and she'd cringed to think of what Rafael's reaction would be. Yet it wasn't her freedom or lack of it she was worried about, she realised—it was Rafael. Something was driving him to act in so domineering a manner, something dark and desperate, and she feared in her impetuous folly she'd made it much worse.

To his credit, Rafael didn't lambast her then. He treated her tenderly, carrying her through the woods, and then calling to Maria to bring cool cloths and compresses and tea as soon as they arrived back at the villa.

The doctor came and looked her over, pronouncing the baby well, the steady thud of his heart on the Doppler wonderfully reassuring. Her ankle was sprained and the doctor bound it up and then gave her strict instructions not to put any weight on it for at least a week, which would undoubtedly please Rafael.

After the doctor had gone Allegra fell asleep,

grateful to retreat into oblivion for a little while
When she woke up Rafael was sitting by her
bed, his head in his hands, his long fingers
driven through his dark, unruly hair. The sight
of him looking so exhausted, so unguarded
made her heart squeeze in a way she wasn't
used to. A shaft of yearning pierced her sweetly,
although what she wanted she couldn't say. To
comfort him, perhaps—but would Rafael ever
accept her comfort? What was between them
now? What *could* be between them?

'Hey.' Her voice sounded scratchy and she
licked her dry lips. She must have become a bit
dehydrated out in the hot sun.

Rafael looked up, his bloodshot eyes widen-
ing at the sight of her. 'You're awake. Here.' He
reached for a pitcher of iced water and poured
her a glass, holding it to her lips.

'Thank you,' Allegra murmured, and drank.
She scooted up in bed, pushing her tangled hair
out of her face as she noted the haggard lines of
his face, the bleak set of his mouth. 'I'm okay,
Rafael,' she said quietly, and to her shock his
face crumpled almost as if he might weep. 'Rafael...' she whispered, reaching out one hand,
and even more to her shock he took it, his fingers interlacing with hers.

'But you could have so easily not been.'

His voice was a ragged whisper as he clung to her hand.

'I behaved foolishly,' she said. 'I'm so sorry.'

Rafael shook his head, the emotion reined in now but still visible in the lines of strain on his face. 'I am the foolish one. You wouldn't have gone off like that if I hadn't driven you to it. If I had been more reasonable.'

'You shouldn't blame yourself...'

'But who else am I to blame?' Rafael returned starkly. 'I am responsible for you, Allegra, and for our child, whether you like it or not. I cannot shirk or ignore that responsibility. I did once before and I will never do so again.'

'When...?' The word was a breath of sound. She realised she wanted, needed to know what drove Rafael. What made him the man he was. She wanted to know so she could understand him, but also so she could comfort him. So she could help. The strength of her own feeling surprised her, but she didn't back away from it. This was too important. *They* were too important. At least she hoped they were.

'My mother,' he said after a moment. 'My sister, in a different way.' He pressed his lips together. 'I lost them both, when it was my sacred responsibility to care for them. I failed them, failed my entire family.' He looked away, blinking fast. 'If I seem too controlling, it's because I can't contemplate the alternative.'

Allegra felt tears sting her eyes at the pain she saw in Rafael's face, heard in his voice. She didn't understand everything but she knew he was hurting. 'I'm sorry,' she whispered, reaching up to brush her hand against his cheek. 'For all you've suffered.'

Rafael closed his eyes, leaning into her brief caress, and then he pulled away. Opened his eyes and didn't look at her. 'In any case,' he said, a stiffness entering his voice, 'I will relax some of the measures I put in place.'

'That still makes me sound like a prisoner.'

'You're not a prisoner.' Now his tone was touched with impatience. Their moment of bonding was well and truly over. 'You're living in the very lap of luxury. I hardly see any reason to complain.'

Allegra tried to tamp down on the frustration she felt rising again. 'Don't *do* that,' she pleaded.

Rafael looked startled. 'Do what?'

'*Change.* One minute you're all solicitude and tenderness and the next you're acting as if you can't spare two minutes to talk to me. It makes my head spin. And it reminds me—' She broke off, biting her lip, and Rafael's eyes narrowed.

'Reminds you of what?'

'My father,' she said after a moment. She leaned her head back against the pillow and closed her eyes. If he'd shared something of his past heartache, then so could she. 'My father because...because after he divorced my mother I never saw him again, as you know.' Her throat thickened and she swallowed hard. 'And before the divorce...he loved me. He acted like he loved me, anyway. He called me his little flower. He tickled me, he tossed me in his arms, he gave me presents and tucked me in at night...' She gave a trembling laugh and brushed at her eyes. 'To have his love, to feel so important, and then to be cut off completely...it was awful, Rafael. The worst thing that ever happened to me.'

'The loss of a father is a very hard thing,' Rafael said after a moment.

'How did you lose yours?'

'He... An accident.' He looked away. 'A terrible accident.'

Allegra wanted to ask more, ask about the history between their fathers, but in that moment she didn't dare.

'Your father left you that necklace in his will,' Rafael said after a moment. 'He must have cared, at least a little.'

'Yes, but I don't even know why he gave it to me.' Allegra smiled sadly. 'There was a note... he asked for my forgiveness, saying he'd cared more for his reputation than for me. But I don't understand that at all.'

'Who can say?' Rafael answered. His voice was guarded, his jaw bunched. Allegra wondered what he knew and wasn't telling. Or was she being paranoid?

'I keep telling myself he really did love me. He must have loved me, but something happened…something that made him act the way he did, cutting us off. But I can't imagine what it was.'

'And I remind you of him.' Rafael sounded cautious and diffident, and realisation scorched through Allegra.

'Only because you keep changing,' she said quickly. 'It's not as if— You don't need to worry, Rafael, I'm not going to fall in love with you or something like that.' She felt herself blush hotly as Rafael jerked back, almost as if she'd slapped him. Clearly the prospect of her falling in love with him was horrifying. Allegra rushed to fill the ensuing taut silence. 'I'm not looking for love,' she hastened to explain. 'I'm not interested…I mean, any…relationship between us wouldn't have to have that. I wouldn't want it to have that. I want us to get along, of course, but…I'm not looking for love, not from you, not from anyone.'

She finally, thankfully, managed to make herself stop speaking. Rafael had sat back in his seat, his expression terrifyingly inscrutable.

'Why not?'

'Because love hurts,' Allegra said simply. 'Doesn't it? To let someone matter that much to you. To let them hold your heart...because hearts can break.' She let out a shaky laugh. 'I sound fanciful, I know, but the truth is I don't believe that old adage about it being better to have loved and lost than never to have loved at all.'

'So you've never been in love? Romantic love?'

'No.' She drew a quick breath. 'Surely you realised that, considering...considering I was a virgin.'

'There's a difference between sex and love.'

'Yes.' Although for her she wasn't sure there was. Her one experience with sex had been far too intense and emotional.

Rafael fastened his resolute gaze on her. 'In any case, we will have a proper marriage.'

A flush swept over her at the thought of what a proper marriage would look like. Feel like. Could she keep herself from loving Rafael, loving the tender, caring man he could be when he wanted to, if she gave her body to him again and again? 'I haven't actually agreed to marry you,' Allegra reminded him.

'Yes, but it's only a matter of time. For our son's sake, Allegra.'

He was so aggravatingly arrogant. Allegra closed her eyes, overwhelmed by it all. 'I asked you to give me time to get to know you,' she said. 'And for you to get to know me. But we can hardly do that when you hide away in your study all the time.'

'I'm not *hiding*,' Rafael snapped.

Allegra opened her eyes. 'Rafael, as soon as you'd brought me here you disappeared. I don't care how busy you are, that's just rude. And cowardly.' His eyes flashed fire and Allegra wondered if she'd gone too far. 'Let's just spend some time together.' Surely there was no real danger in that.

Rafael was starting to look seriously uncomfortable. 'What exactly are you suggesting?'

'An hour or two every day,' Allegra returned. That felt safe. 'Meals spent together. Evenings… some conversation. We had a little bit of that in New York, didn't we?' A very little. 'But you need to stop avoiding me.'

'I'm not avoiding you. I am a busy man.'

'Well?' Allegra pressed, not to be dissuaded. As nervous as she was, she knew she wanted this. 'That's all I want, I promise.'

He leaned forward, his eyes glittering. 'That's all? Are you sure?'

Allegra's breath caught because she recognised the look of ferocious intent in his eyes. Of course she did. She also recognised the hot swirl of longing she felt unfurl inside herself, a languorous warmth that was lazy and urgent at the same time, wrapping her up and making her want. *Him.*

She licked her lips, her throat and mouth turning dry. 'I'm…I'm not ready for that yet, Rafael.'

'The doctor said it was safe.' His gaze roved over her, assessing, probing, demanding.

'That's not what I meant.'

'I know.' He leaned back in his seat, the heat in his eyes turning to a slow simmer. 'But think about it, Allegra. It could be very enjoyable for us both. It *will* be.'

'I…I know.' She had no doubts on that score. How could she, when the memory of their one night together still had the power to scorch her? And yet…the memory of the awful afterwards had the power to scorch as well, in an entirely different and unwelcome way. Things had changed between them since then, but Allegra still didn't trust Rafael—not in that kind of situation anyway. And, she acknowledged, she didn't trust herself.

Rafael's mouth curled in a lazy smile as his

gaze raked over her once more. 'Let me know when you are ready. It will be soon, I think.'

She looked away, unable to stand the heat of his gaze. 'I will,' she answered shakily, and then wondered just what she had promised.

# CHAPTER ELEVEN

RAFAEL STARED UNSEEINGLY at the screen of his laptop as Allegra's words ricocheted around his head, as they had been for the last three days, since she'd said them. *You don't need to worry, Rafael, I'm not going to fall in love with you.*

Words that should have filled him with sweet relief—and they did. Of course they did. But they'd surprised him too, because he hadn't expected such cold, clear pragmatism from her. Allegra was sensitive, emotional, romantic— whether she realised it or not. And yet she'd stated very clearly, with great certainty, that she would never love him. That she *couldn't*. What the hell did that mean anyway? Was that because of her—or him? Because he wasn't worth loving?

It was a question he hated asking, much less answering. It was a foolish, romantic question not worthy of his time. He should be thankful that his wife-to-be was so sensible. So like-minded. Moodily Rafael shut his laptop and gazed out the window of his study instead.

It was a day of lemon sunshine and blue skies, and he was tired of spending it inside. Tired of mulling over everything Allegra had said.

In the three days since their conversation he'd made an effort to spend more time with her. It wasn't always easy, and their conversations were sometimes stilted and jarring, but he had to admit to himself he actually liked being with her. Enjoyed hearing her clear, crystalline laugh, seeing her infectious smile. She'd had much sorrow in her life, but she was made for joy. Joy he wanted to give her, whether it was a gift or a touch…or more. But did she want to receive it? Receive him?

Why was he thinking like this?

The sound of crunching gravel had Rafael rising from his seat. A delivery van was approaching the front of the villa, and he knew what it held. A smile touching his lips, he headed downstairs.

'What is all this?' Allegra asked as the delivery man began bringing in boxes.

'Your things,' Rafael said simply. 'I had everything shipped from your apartment.'

'You did?' She looked flummoxed.

'Did you think we would leave it behind?'

'I don't know. I suppose I did. I knew you were terminating the lease on my apartment.'

'But I thought you'd want your things around you.'

'I do. Of course I do.' She shook her head slowly, smiling at him with a pure radiance that felt like a spotlight on his soul. 'You can be so thoughtful sometimes, Rafael. Thank you.'

'Only sometimes?' he teased. Their banter felt new and fragile, but kind of wonderful too. Allegra's smile deepened.

'Definitely only sometimes,' she teased back. 'But your rate is improving.'

He laughed, and with all of the boxes brought in Allegra began to open them, exclaiming over everything like a child at Christmas. 'My books...my cheese plant!' She looked up at him with laughing eyes, making something in Rafael's chest expand. 'I've had this thing for years, you know.'

'It looks like it needs a little water,' Rafael said, and took it from her. 'It's been in a box for days.'

'Everything came so quickly.'

'Expedited shipping.'

'That must have cost a fortune!' she exclaimed, and he shrugged.

'I can afford it.'

He took the cheese plant to the kitchen and

when he went back to the lounge, Allegra was sitting on the sofa, her cello case in front of her, a thoughtful look on her face. She almost seemed sad.

Rafael propped his shoulder against the door-frame, watching the way her face softened as she opened the case and stroked the buttery-soft wood of the instrument.

'How long have you had that cello?' he asked quietly, and she looked up, blushing at being caught out.

'Since I was nine. My father bought it for me.'

'Did he?' Rafael said quietly.

'Yes…he loved to hear me play.' She let out a soft sigh. 'Even when I wasn't very good, sawing away at it. He'd always clap and say "Bravo."'

'Perhaps you'll play for me sometime,' Rafael said, and saw her eyes flare in surprise. Then she shook her head with sorrowful but firm decision.

'No, I can't.'

Rafael tried to hide the expression of affront and even hurt he feared was on his face. 'I see,' he said, unable to keep his tone from turning cool.

'I haven't played in almost ten years,' Allegra explained. She rested her hand on the cello. 'Not since I was eighteen.'

Intrigued, Rafael straightened. 'Why not?'

She shook her head, her eyes downcast, and he didn't think she was going to answer. 'Because when I was eighteen I auditioned for Juilliard,' she finally admitted on a little sigh. 'Or I should say I tried to audition.' She kept looking downwards as she continued, 'I'd sent an audition tape, and I was invited in for a live audition, which felt huge. It was my dream, to play music. I've taken lessons since I was a small child.' She bit her lip, and Rafael held his breath, waiting.

'It was a big step for me, to send the tape in. I know it might not seem like much, but I was so shy, especially after...well, after my parents' divorce. Music was a personal, even sacred thing to me. It still is.'

'So what happened?' Rafael asked. He felt anxious on her behalf, wanting to hear a happy ending to the story, even though he knew there wasn't one.

'I froze.' She let out a shaky laugh. 'I got there and I couldn't play. It was as if I was paralysed. I literally couldn't do it. The examiners were kind at first, but then they were impatient, and then I was dismissed. And that was that.'

'But why haven't you played since then?'

'I just couldn't. It's as if...I don't know. I just lost it. The desire as well as the ability. If I played now you'd probably cover your ears.'

'I wouldn't,' Rafael said, meaning it utterly.

Allegra stroked the cello again and then closed the case. 'Anyway, silly as it seems, I still like having my cello, so thank you.'

'You're welcome.' Rafael was silent, trying to sift through his emotions—the sorrow he felt for the shy, vulnerable young woman Allegra had been. Empathy, because her father had turned on her just as he'd turned on Rafael's father, his father, and just as with his father, his family, that rejection had had consequences. Protectiveness, too—because he never wanted her to feel that kind of anxiety again. And lastly, stronger than either of those two, desire, different and deeper than any he'd known before. He wanted her to play again. He wanted her to play for him.

But what on earth made him think he deserved such a privilege?

The next week passed in a lovely haze. Allegra felt herself relaxing into everything, especially the time she spent with Rafael. While he still spent a fair amount of time in his study, or going to Palermo on business, he made an effort to make time for her.

One afternoon when Allegra's ankle was feeling better they walked into the nearby hill town to shop at the market. Allegra enjoyed the simple pleasure of inspecting fat, red tomatoes and juicy melons while Rafael followed behind her, a wicker basket looped over one arm.

The ancient, cobbled streets were charming, and the view of the twisted olive trees and dusty valleys below truly magnificent.

Rafael suggested they have a picnic, and so they bought salami and bread, cheese and olives and grapes, and took it all to a stretch of grass overlooking the valley.

'This is wonderful,' Allegra said as she stretched out on the grass and Rafael fed her bread and cheese.

'As long as you don't get sunburned.'

'Don't fuss,' she chided gently, because she knew Rafael was trying, and it tugged at his heart. At moments like this, with everything relaxed between them and the sun shining benevolently above, she felt a marriage between them could work. Maybe it could even be wonderful.

Was she falling in love with him?

The question reverberated through her. When Rafael was kind and gentle and tender, she felt it would be easy to fall in love with him. Easy and amazing. But what if he changed? He had before, and she didn't know whether she could trust him yet. More and more she realised there were reasons Rafael acted the way he did—reasons he hadn't shared with her yet. Although

they'd talked about many innocuous things
he hadn't spoken again of his family, and she
hadn't asked.

Now, lying on the grass, feeling sleepy and
secure, she decided to broach the topic. 'Rafael...what happened between your father and
mine?'

Rafael tensed, his gaze turning guarded.
'Why are you asking that now?'

'Because it seems important. And because the
more time we spend with each other, the more
I want to have no secrets, no hidden things.'

Rafael was silent for a long moment. 'And if
you don't like the answer?' he finally said, his
voice toneless, his gaze shuttered.

Allegra felt the first stirrings of unease. 'Why
wouldn't I?'

'Because your father treated mine unfairly.
Very unfairly.'

Already she was prickling. 'How do you
know—?'

'I know.' His gaze was opaque as he turned
to look at her. 'But even that much is hard for
you to hear.'

'Yes...but that doesn't mean I don't want to
hear it.' Allegra took a deep breath. 'I know he
wasn't perfect. Of course I know that. Look how
he treated me.'

'Yet you're still protective of him.'

'I never wanted to hate him.' She looked away. 'Maybe because I always hoped he'd come back. But he won't now, and I want you to tell me. Please, Rafael.' She held her breath, waiting, and finally Rafael spoke.

'Twenty years ago our fathers were in business together.'

'The mobile technology you mentioned.'

'Yes. Your father provided the science, my father provided the parts. They were partners, friends.' He paused, his expression still shuttered, although Allegra heard the emotion in his voice. Felt the tension in his body next to hers.

'And what happened?'

'Someone embezzled a great deal of money from the company account. Your father blamed mine.'

She searched his face, looking for clues. 'But you don't think it was him?'

'I know it wasn't,' Rafael returned swiftly. 'I know. But your father insisted he had it on good authority, and he let it be known my father was a cheat, even though he couldn't prove it. No one would do business with him any longer. Within months he was ruined, and we were destitute.'

Shock sliced through her, and for a moment she struggled with what to say. How to respond. 'That's why you bought out the company.'

Rafael's mouth firmed. 'Justice was served.'

She sat up, hugging her knees, her mind still spinning. 'Why didn't you tell me this sooner?'

'I didn't know if you would believe me. And,' Rafael admitted, 'I didn't want to hurt you. I knew you loved your father, even if that love was misplaced. Things didn't feel strong enough between us…' He paused, searching her face. 'Do you believe me?'

'Yes,' Allegra said after a moment. 'I do.' And she ached for all Rafael and his family had endured. 'But I also believe that my father must have genuinely thought your father was in the wrong. I don't think he would have acted in such a manner without good cause.'

Rafael made a sound of disgust. 'And do you still think he abandoned you with good cause, Allegra? Why can't you see the man for what he is? *Was?*'

She recoiled, shocked by the vitriol in his voice. 'What does it matter to you if I choose to believe he was a good man?' she demanded stiffly. She felt hurt, and she wasn't even sure why. 'Why can't you let me love him still?'

'Because in my mind he is a demon,' Rafael returned flatly. 'And I will never forgive him.'

They didn't talk all the way back to the villa. The last few days had been so lovely, so promising, and now it all felt flat and strained. Over the last few days she'd actually been starting to care about Rafael. She *still* cared, which was why their argument hurt so much. And, Allegra acknowledged that evening as she lay in bed unable to sleep, it hurt because she know there was truth in Rafael's words. Why did she have to believe her father loved her, when everything pointed to the opposite? Why did she cling to that frail, pointless hope?

Sighing now, Allegra shifted restlessly in bed. The baby kicked, and she placed one hand on her bump, taking comfort from those fluttery movements. Tomorrow they were going to Palermo for a scan, and she was looking forward to the reassurance of an ultrasound, that lovely whoosh of their son's heartbeat filling the air.

But tonight she wasn't thinking about their baby. She was thinking about *them*.

The sudden, soft strains of music floating from downstairs made Allegra still in her restless movements. It almost sounded like...

Holding her breath, she rose from her bed and slipped on the silky wrap that passed for a dressing gown in this hot weather. Even at two in the morning the air inside the villa held a remnant of the day's heat, although the tiles were cool under Allegra's bare feet as she made her way downstairs, following the haunting strains of the cello she heard.

Downstairs all was dark save for a single

lamp burning in the lounge. Allegra hesitated on the threshold of the room; she saw Rafael sprawled in a chair, his long legs stretched out in front of him, his button-down shirt several more buttons open than usual. His hair was rumpled and a tumbler of whisky dangled from his fingertips.

'It's Shostakovich,' Allegra said softly, and he glanced up, his eyes bloodshot and bleary. He was, she realised, a little drunk.

'The third movement of the cello sonata,' he agreed. 'It reminds me of you.'

It was the piece they'd listened to before they'd made love. Allegra was jolted to the core by the fact that he was listening to it now—that he'd remembered, that he cared. 'Why do you need reminding?' she asked softly. 'I'm right here.'

'Are you?' The question hung in the air between them, hovered like a ghost. Rafael gave her a long look before he glanced away, taking a large swallow of his drink.

'Is this about this afternoon?' Allegra asked after a moment. 'Our argument?'

'What do you mean, this?'

'You're sitting downstairs, listening to sad music and drinking whisky.'

Rafael looked away. 'I couldn't sleep.'

'I couldn't either.' She paused, then decided

to up the ante, even if part of her shied away
from being so vulnerable. Admitting so much.
'The truth is, I think you're right, at least partly.
I want to believe my father still loved me because the alternative…' She stopped, catching
her breath, her heart starting to thud. Confes-
sions like this were *hard*. 'The alternative is he
didn't love me, and that means…I'm unlovable.'

Rafael lifted his head to skewer her with a
burning stare. 'You are not unlovable, Allegra.'

'My own father?' She tried to keep her voice
light but it trembled. 'Come on. Parents love
their children. That's a given.'

'Maybe your father was incapable of love.'

'You really think he was a monster,' Allegra
said slowly. Rafael didn't answer. She stared at
him, trying to divine something from the resolute, almost resigned set of his features. 'I don't
want this to come between us, Rafael. Whatever
happened…it's in the past. Let's leave it there.'

'You were the one who wanted to know.'

'And now I do.' She drew a quick breath. 'Is
there anything more? To know?'

A pause, infinite, endless. 'No,' Rafael said
finally. 'Nothing important.'

Allegra supposed she should feel relieved but
she didn't. She felt anxious and also sad because, whatever Rafael had just said, she sensed
that there was still something he was holding

back. She could see it in his face, the set of his shoulders. He was carrying a world of sorrow, and she didn't understand it. She didn't know how to comfort him. But she wanted to.

'Our son is kicking,' she said softly. She pressed both her hands against her bump, laughing a little as their baby kicked against her palm. 'He's a fighter for sure. He's kicking me right now.' She looked up at him, a tremulous smile curving her lips. 'Do you want to feel him?' He hadn't felt their baby kick since that night after the opera. They'd barely touched at all since then. It felt like a lifetime ago.

'Yes.' The single word was certain and utterly heartfelt. Rafael tossed his empty glass onto the table before rising from his chair and coming across the room to kneel in front of her. The warm wash of light caught the bronze strands in his dark hair, the glint of stubble on his jaw. Allegra held her breath, conscious of his closeness, his heat, the yearning inside her to reach him, comfort him. She touched his hair, threading her fingers through its softness, drawing him closer to her.

Slowly Rafael slid his hands along her bump, the warmth of his palms seeping through the thin silk of her nightgown and dressing gown. 'You're bigger,' he said softly. 'Even in just a few weeks.'

'He is growing,' Allegra answered with a little laugh. 'And I'm eating better.'

'You're beautiful,' Rafael answered, his tone almost fierce. 'I've never seen anything so beautiful as you—as this.' His palms curved around her belly, cradling their unborn child. Allegra's heart bumped unsteadily as desire and something deeper flooded through her.

And then their baby kicked, a sharp flutter, almost making her wince. Rafael laughed aloud. 'That was him.'

'Yes.'

'It feels so strong. Stronger than before.'

'Yes, he's quite a kicker.'

'He needs to be strong. He needs to be a fighter, with what's ahead of him.' Allegra thought of the planned surgery, the frightening uncertainty amidst the longed-for news— and the knowledge, sweet and sure, that Rafael would be by her side for all of it. Dependence— trust—could be a wonderful thing.

'Yes. We all have to be strong,' she whispered.

'It will be all right, Allegra.' Rafael's hands continued to cup her belly as he looked up at her, his gaze burning and intent. 'I'll make sure it will be all right.'

Tenderness flooded through her at his fierce expression. She knew he meant every word, and while the future held no promises or guarantees, she believed him. She believed *in* him, in his sincerity, and that faith compelled her to touch her hand to his cheek, her fingers smoothing across the gentle abrasion of his stubbled jaw. 'I know you will, Rafael.'

A brighter light blazed in his eyes and he turned his face so his lips brushed her palm. A shudder went through Allegra; her body shook with the force of it, and her breath came out in a ragged gasp. To be touched again, and so sweetly, so tenderly...

'Rafael...' His name slipped from her lips, and then he opened his mouth and sucked on the tip of her thumb, and her whole body twanged like a bow that had been beautifully plucked. Around them the music swelled, a crescendo of sound to complement the one of sensation Allegra could feel inside her, building, *building*...

Rafael let go of her thumb to turn back to her, and Allegra didn't know who moved first. With his hands on her belly and their baby between them their bodies bumped together, mouths clashing, hands tangling. The kiss went on and on, desperate, urgent and hungry, a symphony whose notes played their sweet music through her body.

Rafael's hands went from bump to her hair

and then to her shoulders and breasts, touching her everywhere, and yet it wasn't enough. She needed him, needed now more than ever to feel the closeness, the connection she'd felt once before. And she thought he needed it too.

Then he pulled away, just a little, but it was enough to make her cry out with the loss of it, of him.

In the shadowy light from the lamp she saw his face, his expression resolute, ready, eyes like fire, a silent question waiting for her yes.

She placed one trembling hand against his chest, felt the steady, comforting thud of his heart. Pressed. Rafael glanced down at her hand, fingers spread out, seeking. He covered it with his own. They remained like that for a suspended second, everything about to tumble into free fall.

And then he bent his head, his lips a whisper away from hers, still waiting for her response. Her yes. And she gave it, leaning forward to kiss him deeply, her hands tangling in his hair, the action a promise, a vow.

He tensed under her hands and mouth, his body like a bow while she was the strings. And then the music began, a glorious symphony, as his hands came up to grip her shoulders hard and his mouth opened under hers, turning her whisper of a kiss into a shout, a plea, a demand—she answered all of them with her mouth, her body, her heart. An offering of everything she had.

His mouth moved on hers as he propelled her across the room and then up the stairs; she stumbled on a step and with a muffled groan against her mouth Rafael scooped her up into his arms, drawing her against his chest. Allegra nestled there, feeling both precious and small, as Rafael carried her easily up the stairs and then down the hall to the master bedroom.

He put her down gently, steadying her as she swayed against him. The room was dark, moonlight spilling through the latticed shutters over the window, and they stood there for a moment, silent, breathing, his hands on her arms.

Allegra couldn't see the expression on his face but she felt the emotion thrum through him as he tightened his grip on her shoulders.

'Are you sure?'

Everything so far had been a resounding and overwhelming yes, and yet still he asked. Allegra placed one hand on his cheek, her thumb smoothing the line of his jaw, learning him, letting him know how sure she was. 'Yes,' she said simply. *'Yes.'*

He didn't ask again. He simply pulled her towards him, his smile gleaming whitely in the dark, and then her clothes fell away; she kicked off her pyjama shorts as Rafael slid her T-shirt over her head.

His breath hissed between his teeth as he looked at her, and Allegra didn't feel self-conscious or big with her belly on display. She didn't feel vulnerable or exposed. Under the heat of his gaze she felt only beautiful.

His hands followed his hot gaze, smoothing over her dips and curves, learning the feel of her with slow, thorough deliberation. She shivered under his touch, his fingers sending sparks along her skin, and then she grew bold enough to touch him, hands flat upon his chest, fingers spreading and seeking the sculpted ridges of his muscles.

'I like that,' Rafael whispered. He remained still under her questing fingers, and with shaking hands she slipped the first shirt button from its hole, and then another and another, until his chest was bare and she was pushing his shirt off his bronzed shoulders, revelling in his body, satiny skin over hard muscle. She hadn't touched him very much that first night. She'd been too overwhelmed by it all, both the pleasure and the grief. Now she revelled in the hot, silky feel of him, running her hand across his chest, down to his abdomen, fingertips brushing the waistband of his trousers.

Rafael let out a groan and Allegra laughed

softly, amazed at how she was able to affect him. Now she felt powerful as well as beautiful.

'You were beautiful before,' he murmured as he reached for her, hands cupping her breasts, thumbs sliding across their aching peaks. 'And you are even more beautiful now, carrying my child.'

'You make me feel beautiful,' Allegra whispered, and then he was bending his head and Allegra slid her fingers through his hair as his lips sought and found her, causing a lightning bolt of pleasure to blaze deep down inside.

He scooped her up again—she felt boneless, weightless—and carried her to the bed. Deposited her on top of the duvet, the silk cover slithering and sliding underneath her. He shucked off his trousers and boxers, leaving her breathless. She'd seen him naked before but the sight still overwhelmed and undid her. He lay next to her and drew her into his arms, their bodies bumping and touching in all sorts of places, making her shudder. It felt so much. She'd known it would; it was why she'd resisted this before, because the intensity felt exquisite and painful at the same time, and she had to brace herself for the tidal wave, to keep herself from falling, drowning.

She'd been telling herself he wouldn't feel the same way, that sex wasn't as important or sa-

red for him, but in that moment as his fingers
touched her face and his body arced into hers
she believed it was. He couldn't touch her like
this, give of himself like this, without it meaning something. She felt it in his kiss, in his gentle hands, in the love he lavished on her body,
finding and plundering all of her secret places.

And then—yes, finally—he was inside her, so
big and right she gasped out loud and he lifted
his head, his gaze blazing down into hers. 'Are
you all right? I didn't hurt you?'

She clasped her legs around him, pulling him
deeper into herself, accepting him fully, feeling complete. 'I'm all right,' she said. 'I'm…'
But she had no words, because the feelings
were coming faster and stronger now, wave
after wave as Rafael began to move and Al-
egra matched his rhythm, reaching, *reaching*…

And finding. Finally, gloriously finding, her
body shuddering with the force of her climax,
Rafael's face buried in her neck as he murmured
words of endearment and promise, their bodies
intertwined in every way possible. How could
you be this close to another human being, Al-
egra wondered, and *not* fall in love?

She tensed, though, as their heart rates slowed
and Rafael, who had been bracing himself above
her so as not to press against her bump, rolled
onto his back. The sudden whoosh of cool air

on her heated skin felt like an unwelcome wake-up call.

What now?

She waited, barely daring to breathe, afraid of this moment and what had it had meant before. Would he dismiss her from his bed? Leave her here alone? Then Rafael reached out one arm and hooked it around her shoulders, drawing her against him so her bump was pressed against his side, her knees snugging into the backs of his thighs. Allegra expelled a silent sigh of relief. It was going to be okay. More than okay.

Gently Rafael caressed her bump, his palm curving around the taut roundness of her belly. He laughed softly as their baby kicked.

'I guess something woke him up.' A smile in his voice, in her heart.

'I guess something did,' she answered, and wrapped her arm around his chest.

# CHAPTER TWELVE

*HE COULD SMELL THE BLOOD. Sharp, metallic. He didn't recognise it, though, didn't understand as he pushed the now broken splintered door open with his fingertips and took a step inside the room.*

*'Papa?'*

*His voice was soft, scared, the voice of a child even though he was sixteen years old.*

*'Papa...'*

*He saw his father's hands first, slack, hanging down, fingers dangling. Then the drops of blood on the desk, a delicate spray, making him think ink had spilled. As if anyone used ink any more, let alone a bottle of bright red. And then his gaze moved upwards and he saw his father's shattered face. Heard a scream rip from his throat—except it wasn't his scream, it was his mother's; she stood behind him, hands raised to her blood-drained face, and the awful unholy sound went on and on.*

'Rafael… Rafael!'

The hand shaking his shoulder woke him up; he came out of the dream like a bullet from a gun, the screaming still echoing in his ears. Next to him Allegra's face was as pale as his mother's had been, pale and frightened.

'Rafael…' she whispered, and he shook off her hand, roughly, and saw her flinch. Hated himself, but he couldn't keep from doing it, from turning away. He swung his legs out of his bed and strode to the bathroom, slamming the door behind him.

In the mirror his face was pale, his forehead beaded with icy sweat. Bile churned in his stomach and he thought he might be sick. Thankfully he swallowed it down, bracing his hands on the pedestal sink as he lowered his head and took several steadying breaths.

He hadn't had that dream in years. A decade, even. He hadn't let himself, had closed that part of his mind right off. *Don't think of it*, because if you did you'd be lost, lost for ever, no coming back. He knew that. Knew if he remembered how he'd begged, begged his father… You couldn't go back from that. You couldn't recover, and so he refused to think of it.

Except, he acknowledged as he looked at his pale reflection in the mirror, he thought of it all the time. Not consciously, but it remained, a

canker inside him, destroying everything good.
Allegra had asked how her father could leave
her, if he'd loved her. Rafael knew the answer
to that in his own case times a thousand.

*Because he didn't love me. Because I couldn't
keep him from destroying himself. Because it's
all my fault.*

He'd seen how his mother had gone, and his
sister too. They'd been swallowed up by their
nightmares, their memories, until there had
been nothing left but a pale husk of a self, and
then nothing at all. He couldn't let it happen to
him. But why the dream, why now?

Slowly he lifted his head and stared at his
reflection. The answer was right there in his
dazed face, the acidic churn in his belly. *Allegra.* Their lovemaking had been both sweet
and powerful, and it had woken up long-dead
parts of him, parts of him that remembered
and felt and feared. Parts of him that he'd iced
over with thoughts of justice, kept frozen with
cold, cold fury. Now everything was waking
up, a spring of the soul, and this was the result.
Dreams he couldn't bear to have. Memories he
didn't dare think about. *Weakness.*

He turned the taps on full blast and washed
his face, scrubbed hard as if it would make a
difference, and then turned them off again. He

stared in the mirror, his eyes opaque, hard, and then he nodded once and left the bathroom.

Allegra was curled up on her side, her back to him, one hand cupping her bump. Thankfully she'd fallen asleep, but even in sleep her face looked sad, her mouth puckered, a frown feathering her brow. Rafael reached out to smooth a red-gold curl away from her cheek and then stopped. No need for that.

Tonight had been intense, and now he needed to get things back the way they had been, comfortable, enjoyable, but not threatening. No danger of scars being reopened, him bleeding again, bleeding right out. Take a step back, make it safe. That was what he needed to do...and preferably without hurting Allegra too much. But hurting Allegra couldn't be his main concern any more. Keeping those memories locked tight away was.

Allegra woke slowly the next morning, blinking in the sunlight streaming from the windows, her body aching in delicious places. For a wonderful moment all she remembered was the pleasure, intense and overpowering, of being with Rafael. The way he'd held her, moved inside her...

Then another memory slammed into the first, leaving her breathless. The nightmare he'd had, the way he'd shut her out. She turned and saw that his side of the bed was empty, the duvet pulled tight across, as if he'd never been there. Had he even come back to bed?

Slowly she got out of bed, sorting through possibilities. What should she do now? How should she act? Despite what they'd shared together last night, she didn't yet know how to handle this moment. Whether to press or pull away. She pulled on the thick terrycloth robe hanging from a hook in the bathroom and then gathered her clothes up, tiptoeing back to her room. Downstairs she could Maria humming in the kitchen, Salvatore's tuneless whistle. Nothing from Rafael.

Back in her bedroom she showered and dressed; her mind sifting through memories, options. What to do? How to feel? Taking a deep breath, she went in search of the father of her child.

She found him in his study, forehead furrowed as he gazed at his laptop, his headphone set dangling from his neck. Allegra stood in the doorway for a moment, an ache in her heart, in her soul. She wanted to walk easily into the room and plop herself into his lap; she wanted to smooth away the furrows on his forehead and kiss that lovely, hard, mobile mouth. She wanted it to feel natural, right, and yet she simply stood there, wondering and waiting.

'Did you have a conference call?' she finally asked, her voice high and nervous as she nodded towards the headset.

Rafael's gaze flicked towards her and then away, revealing nothing. Giving nothing. 'Yes.'

'Are you able to manage most of your business from here?' He'd only gone into Palermo a few times over the last weeks.

'I'll need to start going into Palermo more often.' He turned back to his laptop in a way that felt like a dismissal. 'As well as Rome and Milan.'

'I could come.' She kept her voice light. 'I'd like to come.' Rafael didn't answer, and Allegra took a deep breath. 'Rafael…about last night…'

His mouth tightened, his gaze still on the screen. 'Let's not do a post-mortem.'

'Post-mortem?' Hurt flashed through her. 'Really, that's what you'd call it?'

'You know what I mean.'

'I'm not sure I do.'

Finally Rafael lifted his gaze from his laptop, but then Allegra wished he hadn't. His eyes were opaque, fathomless, hard. 'Last night was pleasurable, Allegra, for both of us. That's all that matters. Let's leave it at that.'

'Rafael…' She took a deep breath, dared. 'What about everything we talked about? What about the dream you had?' As soon as she said

the words she wished she hadn't. An emotion
flashed across his face like quicksilver, gone
before she could decipher it, but she knew it
hadn't been good.

'Forget about that,' Rafael said flatly, and as
he turned back to his screen Allegra knew she'd
truly been dismissed. Still she wouldn't give up
that easily.

'I have a doctor's appointment this afternoon
in Palermo,' she said. 'An ultrasound. Will you
come with me?'

He hesitated, and for that heart-stopping second she thought he wouldn't. That he was turning away from her and their child completely,
for a reason she could not understand. 'Yes,'
Rafael said at last. 'Of course I will.'

Rafael sat tensely by Allegra as the technician
squirted cold, clear gel onto her stomach. They'd
barely spoken on the drive into Palermo, which
should have suited Rafael perfectly but instead
made him feel restless and irritable.

He didn't know what he wanted. The rem-
nants of his old dream still clung to him, ghost
fragments he couldn't shake. They made him
want to keep a little distance between him and
Allegra, but another part of him howled in protest. Hated hurting her…and hurting himself.

'Everything looks good,' the doctor said as

he prodded the ultrasound wand on Allegra's burgeoning bump. 'Baby is the right size...a growing boy.'

The fuzzy black and white shape on the ultrasound screen looked like a proper baby. Head, body, hands, feet, even fingers and toes. He was sucking his thumb and kicking his legs and the sight of him made a pressure build inside Rafael, a pressure he couldn't even begin to understand. His hands curled into fists at his sides and he had to fight to keep his breathing even.

*What was happening to him?*

He felt too much. Happy. Thankful. Afraid. All of it combined inside him, making it hard even to speak. He focused on practicalities instead, helping Allegra up from the table, listening and nodding as the doctor asked them to book another appointment in four weeks' time.

'What shall we do now?' Allegra asked as they left the doctor's office for one of the city's sweeping boulevards.

'Do?' Rafael looked at her cautiously. 'What do you mean?'

'I'm sick of being stuck at the villa,' Allegra said. 'It's lovely, of course, but I've never been to Palermo and I'd like to see it properly. Can we look around a bit?'

Rafael looked at the tremulous hope on Allegra's lovely face and knew he'd have to be a monster to refuse. 'Yes,' he said, the single word drawn from him with reluctance. 'I suppose.'

For the next few hours they strolled down boulevards to squares with sparkling fountains, explored narrow alleys with charming shops and market stalls, and ended up at a café facing the lovely Piazza Pretoria, with its iconic fountain.

Allegra had kept up a steady stream of innocuous conversation the whole time, and Rafael hadn't done much more than offer monosyllabic replies. He was trying to maintain that little bit of distance but it was hard…and becoming harder with every moment.

As they left the café Allegra bent over to reach her bag under the table and the sound of fabric splitting rent the air.

'Oh, no.' She straightened, her face fiery, one hand clapped to her back. 'I've split my skirt,' she whispered, looking mortified, and Rafael looked down at her clothes, realised she'd been wearing the same few loose tops and summer skirts since he'd seen her back in New York.

'I think you need some new maternity clothes,' he said, wishing he'd thought of it sooner.

'I definitely need a new skirt,' Allegra answered, laughing a little. 'I'm not decent!'

'I'll ring a boutique right now.' He draped his

jacket over her as he shepherded her from the café into the waiting limo. Moments later they were stepping into one of Palermo's best boutiques on the Via Liberta, several assistants already waiting to serve them.

Allegra was whisked away to a dressing room while Rafael sat on a white velvet settee, sipping champagne and scrolling through messages on his phone. This was more like it; he could take care of Allegra in the manner he wished to—and that she deserved—without actually having to engage her. She wasn't even in the room.

'What do you think?' Allegra's voice was soft and hesitant and Rafael looked up from his phone, his brain instantly going blank.

Allegra stared at the nonplussed look on Rafael's face and wondered if she'd made a mistake. All afternoon she'd been trying to reach him, keeping up a cheerful one-sided conversation, determined to stay positive.

They'd shared a connection last night. She had to believe that, had to believe it had been real…and that they could have it again.

In the boutique's dressing room she'd tried on several outfits, and then paused when the assistant had given her a sexy, slinky cocktail dress in soft black jersey. This one, she decided, she would show Rafael. See if she finally got some kind of reaction out of him. And now she was standing here, feeling faintly ridiculous, and Rafael was looking blank.

'Well?' She managed a laugh, and then she did a little twirl. 'What do you think?'

'I think…' Rafael cleared his throat. 'I think you look…' He stopped, shaking his head as if to clear it. Allegra smiled. As far as reactions went, she'd take it.

She went back into the dressing room to change while the assistant took her clothes to the shop's till. She was just pulling off the dress when the door opened.

'I think I might need help with the zip,' she said, and then to her shock Rafael answered.

'I think I can do that.'

'What are you doing…?' Allegra began, her breath coming out in a soft sigh as Rafael gently tugged on the zip and then pressed his lips to the nape of her neck.

A shudder went through her and she swayed on her feet, flinging one hand out to brace herself as Rafael's mouth moved down her back.

'Someone will see…' she murmured as he slid the dress further down so it pooled about her hips. She could feel the hard, hot strength of his body behind hers and she leaned back, sagging against him as he kissed the curve of her shoulder.

'No one will see.'

'They'll know.'

'I don't care. I can't see you in that dress and not touch you.'

Touch her but not talk to her. She'd spent all afternoon trying to reach him but it seemed he didn't want conversation. He wanted this.

And so did she.

Rafael pressed against her and Allegra's eyes fluttered closed. *This* was rather wonderful.

'Signor Vitali? We just need your card…' The musical voice of the assistant floated towards them and they both tensed. With what felt like superhuman effort Allegra moved away. She stepped out of the dress and reached for her clothes as Rafael left in search of the assistant.

They didn't speak on the way home, twilight cloaking the mountains in soft violet. Rafael had withdrawn into himself again, his expression shuttered and distant as Allegra curled up in a corner of the limo and dozed.

Back at the villa he disappeared into his office and with a sigh she went to put away her new clothes, sifting through the day's events in her mind. Was she crazy to try to break through the wall Rafael seemed determined on putting up? Foolish to try for more when for her whole life she'd settled for so much less?

Allegra sank onto her bed, her unseeing gaze

resting on the moonlit hills outside the window. She'd come to Sicily because she'd believed it was best for her child. It had felt like a sacrifice, one she had been ready and willing to make.

But now? Now, when she'd felt so much pleasure and happiness and connection with Rafael? When she sensed his overprotective, controlling nature disguised a man who could be tender and loving?

Now she didn't want to come to some *arrangement* where they married and raised their child together, but lived as virtual strangers. Now she wanted a proper husband...and not just in bed.

But how to go about getting it? Was she strong enough to reach Rafael, to keep trying even when he pulled away? To face failure and rejection and keep holding on? She wanted to be. She wanted to make this work.

The click of the door opening had her turning, her surprised gaze arrowing in on Rafael.

'Is everything all right?' she asked uncertainly, because he looked intent and serious and a little sad.

'Now it is,' he said, and relief rushed through her, along with desire, as Rafael came towards her and took her in his arms.

# CHAPTER THIRTEEN

ALLEGRA GAZED AROUND the nursery with a smile of satisfaction. She'd made decorating the room her project over the last week, and she was proud of what she'd accomplished. Pale blue walls with stencilled white elephants cavorting across them, and a cot bed in blond oak with fresh blue sheets ready and waiting, although she didn't actually know when their son would sleep in this room.

The doctors had said he'd be in the hospital for several weeks at least, and then she planned to keep him in a bassinet next to the bed for easy feeding in the night. Still, she was excited about the room, could picture herself in the oak rocker by the window, her son cradled against her chest, sunlight streaming through the window, the perfect picture of familial happiness. Almost.

A sigh escaping her, Allegra moved to the window and looked out at the dusty hills. It hadn't rained in weeks and the air felt stuffy. Now in her sixth month of pregnancy, she felt huge and awkward and more than a little grumpy. She rested one hand on her belly, trying yet again to banish the fears that skirted her mind, threatened to swamp her heart.

For the last few weeks she and Rafael had reached a holding pattern of spending their nights together—and what wonderful nights they were—and the days mostly apart. While she couldn't fault Rafael for his solicitude and kind concern, the remoteness she sensed in him, the careful emotional distance he always kept between them, made her want to scream.

She wanted more. She tried for more, but at every turn Rafael foiled her obvious conversational gambits, her clumsy attempts to increase their intimacy. Was this what love was? Because she thought—she feared—that she loved him. Or at least that she could let him, if he'd let her. If he opened up.

But since that first incredible night he'd stayed remote. He didn't even spend the whole night with her when they made love. He held her for a little while afterwards, but he never slept with her and every morning Allegra woke to an empty bed and an aching heart.

She wanted more than this. She needed more than this. After a lifetime of trying to avoid intimacy and love, here she was, desperate for it. The very situation she'd been wary of had happened, and it felt as if there was nothing she could do about it.

'I have to go to Naples.'

Allegra started in surprise at the sight of Rafael in the doorway of the nursery. She couldn't tell anything from his usual, closed-off expression, but even so she felt a ripple of alarm. 'Naples? Why? Is it business?' He'd gone to Palermo several times a week, and Milan and Rome once each.

There was a slight, taut pause. 'No.'

Allegra frowned. 'No? Then…what? I mean, why?'

Rafael didn't answer for a long moment. Allegra thought he wouldn't. 'My sister,' he said finally, shocking her.

'Your sister…but…' She trailed off, unsure what to say. She'd thought he'd lost his sister, that she'd died. He'd spoken about her as if she was gone, and so Allegra had assumed the worst.

'She's not well,' Rafael said abruptly. 'I need to…go to her.'

Allegra stared at him, sensing the dark undercurrent of anxiety under his terse tone, and she ached to help. Wanted to comfort him, but knew he wouldn't let her. And yet…if he kept her apart in this, what hope was there? How could she ever get closer to him?

'Let me come with you,' she said, part entreaty, part demand, and Rafael's face shuttered.

'No.'

'Why not?' Allegra challenged. 'Please don't keep shutting me out, Rafael, and pushing me away. If we're going to have a child together, if we're going to marry…'

'You are being melodramatic. I haven't pushed you away.'

'Not at night,' Allegra agreed, lifting her chin. 'Not in bed. But in every other way you have. You know you have. I keep trying to reach you, and you keep refusing me. Please, Rafael, don't refuse me in this. I want to support you…'

Rafael stared at her for a long moment, his expression both hard and bleak, and then he finally gave one quick, terse nod. 'Fine,' he said. 'But I need to leave within the hour.'

He shouldn't have let her come. A deep unease settled into Rafael's gut as he climbed into the helicopter after Allegra. He hadn't intended to let her come, of course he hadn't. The last thing he wanted was for Allegra to see Angelica, see his shame.

But, he thought with a resolve tinged with despair, perhaps it was better this way. Perhaps, instead of having to maintain that careful distance, it would yawn between them, gape wide because finally Allegra would see just what he was and how he'd failed.

The call had come that morning, from a doctor in Naples who had found his sister's ID in her bag, as well as his name and phone number. She'd been discovered in an alley, unconscious, unresponsive. The last time the doctor had warned that another overdose could kill her. Angelica didn't seem to care, and Rafael feared that was because she wanted to die. His father's death had been quick, a single shot; his mother a slow, deliberate wasting away. Angelica was choosing self-destruction. And it was all his fault.

'Is your sister ill?' Allegra asked, shouting over the sound of the helicopter that would take them to Palermo for the short flight to Naples.

'In a manner of speaking.' Rafael turned to look out the window to avoid answering any more of Allegra's questions. She would see soon enough what Angelica was like. What he was like.

*And then?* The unease he'd been feeling deepened into dark regret. Then things would be changed between them for ever.

They didn't talk much on the flight to Naples; Allegra seemed to sense his mood and kept quiet, while Rafael kept his head down, his eyes on his tablet, dealing with work issues.

A car was waiting for them when they emerged from the airport, blinking in the afternoon sunlight, the muted roar of the city's traffic, the raucous honking of horns and exclamations of passers-by hitting Rafael like a smack in the face. He didn't like the busy, dirty streets of Naples. He'd offered a dozen times or more to pay for Angelica to move somewhere more congenial, but she'd always refused.

He gave the address of the hospital to the driver and then leaned back in the seat. Allegra looked at him in concern.

'Won't you tell me what's going on?' she asked quietly.

'What is there to tell?' Rafael shrugged, dismissing the question with a lift of his eyebrows. 'My sister is in hospital.' He paused, pressing his lips together. 'A drug overdose.'

He could tell he'd shocked her with that one. And that was just the beginning.

'What…?' Allegra's face crumpled with sympathy. 'Oh, Rafael…'

'Don't.' He shrugged away her compassion. 'It happens often enough. And there's nothing I've been able to do about it.'

Allegra lapsed into silence and Rafael looked

away. He really shouldn't have brought her, but perhaps it would, painfully, be for the best.

Allegra's mouth was dry, her heart pinging in her chest, as she followed Rafael into the hospital lift. He pressed a button and then folded his arms over his chest, biceps bulging, face like an iron mask.

She'd been surprised and gratified when he'd agreed to let her come, but since he'd made that decision he'd seemed only to regret it, and he'd been colder and more remote that ever. She wondered if asking to come had been a mistake, and if Rafael would simply use this as a way to push her even further away.

The doors of the lift opened and Rafael strode out, while Allegra hurried to keep up. Then he was tapping perfunctorily on the door of a room before opening it and slipping inside. Allegra followed him.

The woman in the bed was asleep, dark lashes sweeping gaunt cheeks. Allegra stifled a gasp at the heart-wrenching sight of her—scars on each wrist and bruises and needle puncture marks scoring her arms in dozens of places. Her hair was dirty and tangled, her limbs scrawny, tendons sticking out like ropes. Rafael let out a shuddering breath. The woman's eyes fluttered opened and then focused on Rafael.

'You shouldn't have come,' she rasped out, her eyes burning like coals as she glared at him.

'Of course I came.' Rafael gazed at her for a moment, his expression closed and yet his eyes full of pain. 'Why, Angelica?'

Angelica shook her head, her eyes closed again. 'I don't want to talk to you.'

'Let me help you,' Rafael said, his voice taking on a strident edge. 'Please. There is a room waiting at the best clinic in Europe, in Switzerland. It's luxurious, Angelica, and discreet. You'd want for nothing.'

Angelica shook her head again, without opening her eyes. Allegra's heart started to splinter. She hated seeing Rafael like this, knowing how helpless, how hopeless, he must feel.

Rafael pressed his lips together, staring at his sister in a heart-breaking mix of grief and fury. 'I've only wanted to help you, Angelica. That's all I've ever wanted.'

Angelica opened her eyes, and Allegra stifled a gasp at the hatred and anger she saw in their depths. 'Help me? When have you ever *helped* me?' she demanded in a raw and ragged voice. Rafael flinched but didn't reply. Didn't defend himself. 'Do you know what he did?' Angelica demanded, turning to Allegra. She stared, speechless, unsure how to respond, how to feel.

'Do you?' Angelica's voice rung out. Allegra licked her lips.

'I...I don't...'

'He killed our father,' Angelica spat. 'He *killed* him. My brother only ever thought of himself. He didn't...he couldn't...' She turned away, sobs tearing her chest.

Allegra had no idea what to say. She didn't believe Angelica, the words of a vindictive and desperate drug addict, and yet...

Why wasn't Rafael saying anything?

'You can't deny it, can you?' Angelica said, her voice still coming in ragged gasps.

'No,' Rafael said after a moment. 'I can't.'

Shock rippled through Allegra. Rafael shot her a cold, hard glance. 'Now you know,' he said, but Allegra didn't feel she knew anything.

'Leave me,' Angelica demanded in a low voice. She seemed drained, lifeless. 'Leave me, I beg of you.'

Rafael gazed at his sister for a full minute while Allegra watched, her heart thudding in her chest. Then he turned and walked out of the room.

Allegra followed, her heart aching now, everything aching. 'Rafael...' she began when they'd entered a small waiting room, but he shook his head.

'Don't. I shouldn't have brought you here.'

'I asked to be brought here,' Allegra answered. 'I want to share your sorrows along with your joys. Please, Rafael…'

Rafael just shook his head again, pacing the small waiting room like a panther in a cage.

'How long has she been like this?' Allegra asked quietly.

Rafael didn't still his stride. 'Since she was fifteen. A year after my father died.'

'How…how did he die?'

He lifted his tormented gaze to hers, his mouth twisting. 'You heard her.'

'I don't believe her.'

'Don't you?'

'No,' Allegra said, but her voice wavered. She didn't believe Angelica, not really, but she knew something had happened, something that tormented Rafael, that made him the way he was, dark and distant, and she was afraid to find out what it was.

'Well, you should,' Rafael said, and turned away.

'Why don't you tell me your version?' Allegra asked quietly. 'What really happened?'

'What really happened?' He stopped, raking his hands through his hair and then dropping them in one abrupt movement. 'My father killed himself. I was the last to see him.'

Uncertainty mingled with sorrowful relief rushed through her. 'Then you didn't kill him...'

'I drove him to his suicide. And then I wasn't able to stop him from pulling the trigger.'

'Oh, Rafael...'

'And my mother and my sister blamed me. They blamed me, and they should have blamed me, because...because I couldn't...'

'But it wasn't—'

'You know what I was saying to him before he killed himself?' Rafael didn't wait for her to reply, not that she had any idea what to say. 'I was complaining about having to leave my private school, because there was no more money. My father had lost everything, everything, and I was whinging about school.' He shook his head slowly.

'Rafael, you were a boy...'

'A stupid, selfish boy. And it broke my father. He left the room and locked himself in his study...' He stopped, shaking his head again. 'But there's no need to talk of it. Angelica won't see me again. You might as well return to the villa. I never should have brought you in your condition.'

'I'm not an invalid.' Her heart was aching, aching for this man she loved. And yet Rafael's expression was stony, and when she reached out a hand he jerked away from her.

'I'll arrange your flight.'

'What…what about you?'

Rafael shook his head. 'I won't come with you. I have business to see to.'

Allegra stared at him helplessly, knowing that Rafael was taking another step away from her, and this one far worse than any before. Yet what could she do?

'Please don't do this, Rafael,' she whispered, but he was already getting out his phone.

It was better this way. Rafael continued to tell himself that as he arranged Allegra's flight and saw her onto it. She looked at him with a face full of hurt and desperation, but he steeled himself against it.

She might want to make explanations, excuses, but he couldn't. And he wasn't about to open either of them to more pain. What it meant for their future, he didn't know. But now he knew he needed distance. Space.

He stayed in Naples for another two days, trying to reason with Angelica, but she wouldn't even talk to him. He called Allegra, and was reassured she had returned safely to the villa.

'When are you coming back?' she asked, her voice soft and sad.

'I don't know,' Rafael answered tersely. 'I have business in Milan and Rome.'

'I miss you,' Allegra said quietly, and he didn't answer. But after the call he spent several long minutes staring out the window at the dark night.

'I miss you too,' he said into the empty silence of his hotel room.

# CHAPTER FOURTEEN

THE NEXT WEEK WAS ENDLESS. Allegra drifted around the villa, wishing she could make things better and feeling utterly powerless. She went over her conversation with Rafael again and again, considering all that he had and hadn't said.

Did he really blame himself for his father's suicide? If anyone, she thought with a bitter pang, he should blame her father, for ruining his. No wonder Rafael had been so driven to see justice served. His family had been utterly destroyed.

But *they* didn't have to be destroyed. She couldn't let this ruin them, and yet Rafael seemed hell bent on letting the past destroy any chance of their future.

She thought she understood now why he'd been so distant these last few weeks. Not because he didn't care but because he cared too much…at least, that's what she hoped. She hoped that it was fear of getting hurt that was keeping him away rather than brutal indifference.

Because that's how she'd felt for so long. Loving someone was risky. Loving *hurt*, because people left you. People hurt you. And Rafael didn't want to be hurt.

She hadn't either. She'd lived her life for safety's sake, never letting anyone get close, missing out because it was easier. Safer. But she didn't want to do that now. Now she wanted to risk. Now she was willing to risk everything, because she knew she loved Rafael. And love risked. Love fought. Love, she hoped and prayed, won. But first Rafael had to come back.

Rafael unlocked the front door, every muscle aching with weariness. He'd spent the last week working as hard as he could, in a desperate and fruitless effort to forget. To erase the memory of Allegra, the sweetness of her, so he'd be strong enough to come back here and maintain his distance. Stay separate.

It was late and the villa was swathed in darkness, everyone hopefully in bed. Rafael intended to creep quietly to his bedroom and avoid Allegra altogether. He'd barely taken a step before he heard a creak on the stair and then he turned to see Allegra standing there.

Her hair was tumbled about her shoulders and she wore a silky white slip of a nightgown that left frustratingly little to the imagination. Already desire was surging through him, and he wondered if he could make this simple. If he could make it about sex.

Then she took a step forward, one pale, slender hand held out in appeal. 'Rafael,' she said softly, and he tensed because there was no supplication in her voice. No accusation. There was just warmth. Acceptance. He turned away.

'I thought you'd be asleep.'

'I've been waiting for you.'

'You didn't even know I was coming back tonight.'

'I know.' She let out a soft, sad laugh. 'I've been waiting since you left, Rafael. A whole week.'

His chest felt tight and he tried to shake the feeling off. 'You shouldn't have.'

'Why not? Why are you pushing me away?'

'Why aren't you pushing me away?' The words burst out of him, revealing, and yet he couldn't keep himself from it. He turned to her, his voice ragged, his gaze burning. 'Why are you still here?'

She looked hurt, shocked. 'Do you want me to leave?'

'No.' He scrubbed his eyes with the heels of

his hands. Something felt broken deep inside him and he couldn't articulate what it was, even to himself. 'I'm getting a drink.'

He stalked into the lounge, and after a taut moment Allegra followed him. Rafael poured himself a large measure of whisky from the crystal decanter and drank it down in one healthy swallow. He could feel Allegra's presence behind him. He could feel her confusion and hurt. 'You should go back to bed.'

He heard a sound, something he couldn't quite identify. She was moving or opening something, and he didn't know what it was. He stayed with his back to her, willing her to leave him alone even as a deeper part of him ached for her to stay.

Then he heard the first sorrowful note hover in the room, steal into his soul, and shocked blazed through him. She was playing the cello.

He turned slowly, his glass dangling from his slack fingertips as he took in the sight of Allegra, her hair tumbling about her shoulders in a fiery halo, her expression serious and intent as she drew the bow across the strings of the cello and another sonorous note flowed through the room.

'But…' His voice was hoarse, breaking the stillness. 'You said you didn't play. Hadn't played for ten years.'

Her gaze lifted and something deep in him trembled at the expression in her eyes, silvery and huge, clear and full of sadness. Full of *love*.

'I haven't. But I want to play for you, Rafael. Music…' She paused, her voice choking. 'Music has been the greatest comfort to me. And I don't know of any other way to comfort you.'

She bent her head again and began to play once more, the notes sure and true and piercingly beautiful.

Rafael's throat thickened with emotion and he sank into the sofa as the music washed over him, note after perfect note, the music haunting and powerful, *breaking* him. He was broken inside, nothing but jagged pieces, his heart a handful of splinters. He let out a sound, a choking cry that would have shamed him if he hadn't felt so overwhelmed.

Allegra kept playing, each note touching his soul, undoing him. He let out another choked sound, and then Allegra was kneeling there in front of him, her arms around him, her face pressed against his chest as she whispered words that felt like sweet, sweet arrows, piercing the armour he'd surrounded himself with for so long.

'I love you, Rafael. I *love* you. Nothing matters to me but that. But you. Please believe me. *Please*.'

He let out a groan, defenceless against the onslaught of her heartfelt words. 'How can you love me…?' The words spilled from him, heedless.

'How can I not?' She pressed her lips against her jaw. 'I fell in love with you the night of my father's funeral.'

'I was only trying to seduce you…'

'And I wanted to be seduced. I saw glimpses then of the man you really are, the man you want to be. Don't turn away from me now, simply because you're afraid.' She laid her hand against his jaw, her skin silky and cool. 'Because that is why you've been keeping your distance, isn't it, these last few weeks, and even more so since we went to Naples? Because you're afraid of being hurt.'

He closed his eyes, not wanting to admit it, knowing it was true. He'd tried to separate his body from his heart but it hadn't worked. Allegra affected him in every way, right down to his core. And yet still he found himself saying, 'I didn't think anyone would love me. That anyone could love me…after my father…' He shook his head, his eyes closed, and Allegra kissed him again, her lips soft against his jaw. 'How could he do that? How could he walk away from me and kill himself? I begged him, Allegra. Pleaded with him with everything I had, pounded on the door, and still he did it, knowing the cost of it on me, on my mother and sister. How could he do that?'

The question rang out, the cry of a hurt child. It had festered inside him for twenty years, until his heart was nothing but scar tissue, barely healed over the old, old wound. And Allegra, and her love, had broken it all—him—open.

'I asked you something similar,' she whispered, her lips moving against his cheek. 'Do you remember? And you told me it wasn't my fault. Now I say the same thing to you, only even more so. Your father was a desperate man, Rafael, driven to terrible things because—because of my father. It wasn't your fault, just as my father leaving wasn't mine. Let's leave the past behind us and make our own future, for the sake of our child and for the sake of us.'

'But it was my fault,' Rafael groaned, his voice breaking on the word. 'Not his death, perhaps, but my mother…my sister…the choices they made, the fact that they felt compelled to make them. That they didn't trust me to provide for them, to see us through the darkness and the mess. *That* was my fault. I was the man of the family, I was in charge, and I failed utterly. I can't forgive myself for that. How can anyone else?'

\* \* \*

Allegra squeezed Rafael's hands, holding on tight, wanting to imbue him with her strength, her love, because she felt as if everything teetered on this moment. Whether he would pull away for good or if the walls would finally come down for ever.

She recognised the core of honour and compassion that he'd kept hidden for so long, realised now that his withdrawal from her had not been from indifference but because he'd cared too much.

She knew that he now suffered from both guilt and hurt—just as she did, with her father's abandonment. Because when you were hurting, you assumed it was something in you that drove a person away. Something bad or wrong. And she would give anything now to show Rafael that there wasn't.

Slowly she leaned forward, still holding his hands, her bump pressing against him as she brushed her lips across his in a kiss of acceptance and healing. A kiss where she offered her whole self, there for the taking.

His body was still, his lips slack under hers, and her heart trembled at the terrible thought of his rejection, but then he opened his mouth and made the kiss his own, one hand coming to rest on the back of her head, and he took what she offered and gave even more back.

Moments later they broke apart and with a shuddering breath Rafael leaned his forehead against hers. 'When my father died,' he murmured, his breath fanning her face, 'I felt like my world had shattered…not just because we lost everything but because I'd lost him. Because he'd been driven to such despair, and I couldn't stop it. Couldn't stop him.'

'I'm so sorry, Rafael…'

'I felt powerless and out of control. And I never wanted to feel like that again. But then I cruelly inflicted that pain on another family. I killed your father too, Allegra.'

'What are you talking about?'

'If what Caterina said was true…then your father died of a heart attack when he heard the news about me taking over the company. I killed him—'

'No, you didn't,' Allegra said quietly. 'You can't know exactly what happened, and in any case you can't blame yourself for my father's death along with everyone in your family.'

His eyebrows rose in disbelief. 'You absolve me?'

'I'm not the one to do that, Rafael. You don't need my forgiveness.'

'Whose then?' The question was genuine, yearning.

'Your own,' Allegra said softly. 'Rid yourself of these ghosts and demons. Your father chose to kill himself—there was nothing you could have done. Despair leads people to feel there's no way out, no hope. That was not your fault.' He opened his mouth to protest but she continued, her voice rising in strength and conviction. 'And your mother—that was her choice too. Perhaps she didn't want to live without her husband. It's not a reflection on you—'

'It is—'

'*No.* Maybe she should have wanted to live for her children, but some people are not strong enough. Don't blame her, Rafael, but don't blame yourself either. For your mother's death or your sister's addiction.'

'And your father?' Rafael asked after an endless moment of silence. 'Don't you…aren't you angry for what I did?'

*Was she?* 'I understand why you wanted to take over his business,' she said slowly. 'And I wish I understood more fully what happened back then. Did my father blame yours on purpose, knowing he was innocent? Who else could have embezzled the money?'

Rafael stiffened. 'It wasn't my father.'

'I know,' Allegra soothed. 'And maybe we'll

never know who was truly responsible. But let's put it behind us, Rafael. For ever.'

He stared at her, and Allegra held her breath, waiting, everything in her aching. She'd given him everything. Her love, her heart, her body, her soul, her music. Everything. And she still didn't know what he was going to do with it.

'I want to try,' Rafael said at last, and Allegra nodded as she blinked back tears.

'Yes,' she said. 'Let's try.'

# CHAPTER FIFTEEN

THE REALISATION WAS like a thunderclap, startling her awake. Allegra stiffened in bed, her heartbeat coming in thuds. Next to her Rafael slept on. They'd gone to bed together, holding hands, silent and accepting. It felt like a new start, fresh and fragile. Allegra hoped it would endure. That they would.

And then, in the midst of sleep, she'd had that sudden thought slam into her, leaving her breathless and reeling. *Her mother.* Her mother had embezzled that money. It made such horrible sense. Someone close to her father had taken the money; that same person had pointed the finger at Rafael's father. And it made her parents' sudden divorce understandable too, along with the lack of alimony, her father's concern for his own reputation. But where had the money gone?

Although Jennifer had always claimed poverty, after the divorce they hadn't been exactly destitute. It wasn't as if they'd been out on the streets. Looking at the situation now, a grown woman, Allegra doubted that a few pieces of jewellery could have really kept them afloat. Even the embezzled money wouldn't have lasted long in Jennifer's hands—the woman was a spending machine—but it would have tided them over for a while...until she'd found another man to fund her lifestyle. It seemed, all of a sudden, entirely, horribly possible.

If it was true...what would it mean for her mother—but far more importantly, for her and Rafael?

Allegra slipped from the bed, throwing on a dressing gown before reaching for her laptop. She typed in the Internet search box and within seconds she had the dates of both Marco Vitali's suicide and her parents' divorce. Weeks apart. *Weeks.*

Allegra pushed the laptop away as she stared unseeingly into the distance, her mind racing. If her mother had taken the money...if her father had discovered it...if he'd divorced her so abruptly because of that, wanting to separate himself from his wife but unwilling for his reputation to suffer...

There was only one way to find out. One way to truly know. She needed to talk to her mother. Allegra toyed with the idea of a phone call but she knew she wouldn't be able to get the truth over a telephone line. She needed to see her mother face to face, and see the truth, or lack of it, in her eyes. She needed to know. Because perhaps then she and Rafael could finally put the past to rest and move on as a family. Perhaps then he could find the closure he so desperately needed.

She glanced back at him, his face relaxed in sleep, his dark lashes feathering his olive-toned cheeks. He looked beautiful, like something out of a Renaissance painting, and he made her heart ache with love. But would he countenance a trip to America? What would his reaction to the possibility of her mother's crime be?

As if he could sense her thoughts Rafael opened her eyes. He blinked away the dazed confusion of sleep, his amber gaze arrowing in on her. 'Allegra? Is something wrong?'

She licked dry lips, her heart starting to pound. What if he was angry? What if he blamed her somehow? Despite everything they'd said and shared, she still didn't know if Rafael actually loved her. He hadn't said the words. He'd fought against the feeling, even last night, everything in him resisting, but she'd pressed and pushed and tried so hard...

'Allegra?' Rafael said again, his tone sharpening.

'I think I know who embezzled the money. Back then.'

'*What?*' Rafael sat up in bed, his eyes narrowed as he raked a hand through his hair. 'How could you possibly know that?' He almost sounded suspicious. Of *her*.

Allegra took a deep breath. She felt nervous, even afraid. Why was she risking this— *them*—so soon? Before she even knew the truth or strength of Rafael's feelings? And yet, with this new truth lodged inside her like a stone, how could she not?

'It came to me last night.' She gulped, Rafael's stare still hard and unrelenting. 'I think... I think it was my mother.'

'Your *mother*?'

'It makes sense, in an awful way. She had some money, but she didn't get it from my father. And the divorce was so sudden, so abrupt...'

Rafael swung his legs out of bed, sitting so his back was to her, his hands raked through his hair.

'This doesn't have to change anything between us,' Allegra said quietly. 'Does it?'

'There's no proof, is there?' Rafael's voice was flat, toneless. 'We could never prove it.'

'I...I don't know. I thought, perhaps, we could go to New York. Confront her. Maybe...maybe then you'd feel...' She trailed off, uncertain and miserable. Why had she begun this wretched conversation? Yet she couldn't have kept such an awful suspicion, a huge secret, to herself. She didn't want there to be secrets or lies between them, ever.

'You can't go to New York in your state.'

'Rafael, I'm barely into the third trimester. And I want to be there. Let's do this together. Even if there's no proof, it would be good to know, wouldn't it? Maybe then…maybe then you could finally let the past go.'

'While your mother walks free?'

Allegra blinked at the savage note in his voice. 'I'm sorry,' she whispered, because she was, even if none of it was her fault. Still everything felt complicated and messy, painful.

'I'll book the tickets,' Rafael said, and then he rose from the bed and walked out of the room.

It felt like too much, on top of everything that had happened last night. Allegra's *mother*. She'd as good as signed the death warrant on his family. He didn't blame Allegra, knew she had nothing to do with it, and yet…

It felt bitter, almost too much to bear.

Rafael got ready in taut silence, booking the tickets, packing clothes, telling himself he'd feel better when he knew.

Salvatore drove them to Palermo; Allegra looked tired and miserable, huddled on one side of the limo, one hand resting on her bump. Guilt flashed through him, an acidic rush. She'd given him so much last night. She'd told him she loved him. And he'd fought her every step of the way, couldn't bear the thought of being that vulnerable. That exposed.

And yet he'd shown her the worst of him and she still hadn't walked away. Even now, when he was practically ignoring him, Allegra was there, for the duration, determined to stay by his side, to see this through.

And maybe she needed this as much as he did. If her mother was guilty, it had affected Allegra's life as much as his. They'd both been ensnared by the past—and perhaps the truth could now set them *both* free.

The thought was radical, shifting truths inside him, tilting the world so his perspective was sharper, clearer.

Rafael reached over and took Allegra's hand; surprise flickered across her face as he laced his fingers through hers. He didn't speak; he didn't think he had the words. But he hoped she knew what he was trying to say.

The city was resplendent with autumn colour as they took a cab from the airport to Allegra's mother's apartment in the less fashionable end of Park Avenue, skirting Harlem. Allegra had slept for much of the flight, taking comfort from Rafael's silent support. He hadn't said much, but the mood had shifted between them, the tension focused outward rather than inside. Allegra rested her hand on his shoulder as she dozed and prayed that this would be what she wanted it too—closure. Peace.

Jennifer's expression was almost comical in its shock as she took in the sight of both of them standing in the doorway of her apartment. Her hand fluttered towards her throat and her face paled. 'Allegra...and you must be Vitali.'

'Rafael Vitali,' Rafael answered in a low, gravelly voice. 'Marco's son.'

'I never met him.' Jennifer's expression had cleared, hardened. She was, Allegra realised with a sinking feeling, going to put up a front.

'Mother, may we come in?'

'Of course. Have you...have you come all the way from Sicily?'

'This very afternoon,' Rafael answered. They followed Jennifer into her sitting room where she perched on a white leather sofa, eyebrows elegantly arced.

'What a lovely surprise.'

'Is it?' Allegra asked quietly, and Jennifer's eyes narrowed.

'What is that supposed to mean?'

Allegra took a deep breath. 'Mother, Marco Vitali was accused of embezzlement and lost his business as a result.'

'I told you that,' Jennifer answered with a dismissive flick of fingers. She shot Rafael a quick, wary glance. 'I'm sorry for it, of course, but it has nothing to do with me.'

'He killed himself as a result.'

Jennifer's expression didn't change. 'Again, I'm sorry.'

'There was never any proof it was him, though,' Allegra continued, determined to see this through. She and Rafael both needed to have this reckoning. 'The only so-called proof was that someone close to Papa told him it was Marco.'

Jennifer shrugged her bony shoulders. 'So?'

'So, who was that person? And who really did take the money? Because it was someone close to my father, someone he trusted.'

'You flew all the way to New York to talk about this?' Jennifer demanded, her lips twisting in a sneer. 'I suppose he put you up to it?' she added with a glare at Rafael.

'I did not,' Rafael returned, his voice a low thrum in his chest. 'In fact, I did not want her to make the trip in her condition. But I realised I did want to know. Not for my sake,' he emphasised, his voice lowering to a growl of menacing intent, 'but for Allegra's.'

'What…?' Allegra turned to him, her lips parting in wordless shock.

'If your mother is guilty,' Rafael said, 'then she affected your life as much as mine.' He turned to Jennifer, skewering her with a gaze full of knowledge and accusation. 'Because that's why her father stayed away, isn't it? You made him.'

Jennifer's mouth dropped open and for a few seconds she struggled to speak. 'I don't know what you're talking about,' she finally blustered.

'No,' Rafael answered, so firm, so sure. 'You do know. Because you tried to use Allegra as a bargaining chip.'

'What?' Allegra's mind raced. 'How do you know…?' she demanded of Rafael, the words torn from her.

'I don't. I'm guessing.' He nailed Jennifer with a look. 'And I'm right.'

Jennifer glared at him for a full minute, and then she rose from the sofa, flouncing over to the bar where she poured herself a stiff drink. Allegra watched her, her heart seeming to beat its way up her throat.

'Mother, is that true? Did you threaten Papa? Is that why—?'

'You always thought your father was a saint,'

Jennifer said as she tossed back her drink in one swallow and then flung the glass on the table. 'Even when he walked away from you for good.' She turned around, her arms folded tightly against her chest. 'You can't prove anything. There's no paper trail, nothing. Trust me on that.'

'So you did do it,' Allegra cried, tears streaking down her face. 'How *could* you...?'

Jennifer pressed her lips together. 'Your father kept me on very short purse strings.'

'But why did Papa leave...?'

She looked away. 'I told him if he made me leave he'd never see you again. He didn't want to go through the courts, didn't want the stain on his precious reputation. To have a criminal for a wife! He couldn't bear it. And I thought... I thought he'd change his mind, if he couldn't have you. I didn't know he'd be so bloody stubborn.'

Allegra leaned back against the sofa cushions, her whole body weak and trembling with shock.

'I never meant Vitali to be blamed the way he was,' Jennifer said defensively. 'I just suggested it once. I didn't expect Vitali's business to be ruined by it.'

'You destroyed the life of an entire family,' Allegra said, her voice shaking. '*You* have blood on your hands.'

'Is it my fault that he chose to do that?' Jennifer cried. 'He didn't have to.'

'No, he didn't,' Rafael interjected quietly. To Allegra's surprise he didn't look as angry as she expected him to. He looked sad and resolute, and the surest rock upon which she could depend. He put his arm around her, drawing her close to him. 'You are not to blame for his death,' he said to Jennifer. 'But you are a criminal all the same, and you know it.'

Jennifer's eyes shot sparks as she lifted her chin and said nothing. 'Tell me,' Rafael said quietly. 'Did Mancini ever try to contact Allegra?'

Jennifer looked as if she wasn't going to answer. 'There were letters,' she said finally, and looked away.

Allegra let out a gasp. '*Letters...* Did you keep them? Why didn't you show them to me?'

'I could hardly do that,' Jennifer dismissed. 'You would have started asking questions. But I'm not completely heartless, you know.' She pressed her lips together, and then she turned on her heel and walked out of the room.

Allegra pressed her cheek against Rafael's chest and he put his arms around her. 'How did you know…?' she whispered.

'I guessed.'

'I never thought…never imagined…'

'Maybe now you'll find some answers.'

Allegra look up at him, her eyes wet with tears. 'I already have, Rafael. With you. In you.'

A brief, trembling smile touched his lips and he rested his forehead against hers. Allegra closed her eyes.

'I'm so sorry to interrupt this touching scene,' Jennifer said. She tossed a packet of letters on the table in front of them and Allegra took them up, scanning the faded envelopes. There had to be at least a dozen.

'We'll go now,' Rafael said, rising from the sofa.

'Wait.' Allegra touched his sleeve. 'Don't you have anything to say to Rafael?' she demanded of her mother. 'Do you know how much he has suffered? His family has suffered?'

Jennifer flinched a little but then pressed her lips together and said nothing. She wouldn't admit any more guilt than she had to.

'It doesn't matter, Allegra,' Rafael said quietly. 'This isn't about me.'

'But it is—'

'No.' He cut her off with gentle firmness. 'This was about you. You needed to hear this.' He gestured to the letters. 'You needed to see this.' He tugged her up to standing, his gaze intent and full of—dared she believe it?—love. 'And now we can truly move on.'

Moments later they were standing in front

of her mother's building, blinking in the bright sunlight. Allegra pressed her father's letters to her chest as she shook her head in wonder.

'I never expected this…'

'I'm glad it has happened.'

'But what about you, Rafael? Does it…does it matter, knowing my own mother…?'

'Someone I love taught me that the sins of our parents do not have to affect or define us. The past doesn't have to destroy our future.'

A tremulous smile bloomed across her face, planted its roots deep in his heart. 'Do you mean that?'

'I love you, Allegra. I've loved you for a while, but I fought it because I am a blind, hard-headed fool. And I was afraid, just as you guessed and said. Afraid of being hurt. Of seeming weak. But you saw all my weakness and failure and you loved me even then. Even more.'

'I love you,' she said. '*All* of you.'

'And I love all of you.' He put his arms around her and drew her to him. 'Especially since you can forgive me when I act so foolishly, pulling away when I should have pushed closer.'

'I understood it was scary, Rafael. It was scary for me too.'

'But you wised up a lot faster than I did,' he said with a smile. He brushed his lips across hers. 'Now let's go home.'

# EPILOGUE

*Eighteen months later*

'HE'S THE SMARTEST baby that ever was,' Allegra declared.

'Of course he is,' Rafael answered easily, as he joined her on the lawn, stretching his long legs out on the blanket. The sunshine bathed them in a golden glow, and above them the leaves rustled pleasantly. Their son, named Marco after Rafael's father, babbled excitedly as he attempted to heft his chubby self to his feet.

'He's trying to walk,' Allegra exclaimed. 'And the doctors said he wouldn't walk until he was at least two.'

'Yes, but what do they ever know?' Rafael teased.

It had been a long, hard year and a half in many ways. Little Marco had spent four months in the neonatal unit, first getting strong enough to handle heart surgery and then recovering from that surgery. There had been a few scary moments along the way—a bout of pneumonia that had tested his lungs, and an infection after his surgery. But he'd grown stronger and stronger and finally, when their son had been nearly five months old, they'd brought him back to the villa to begin their life together as a proper family.

Three months ago they'd got married, a small, intimate ceremony in the nearby town, with only a handful of guests. Allegra hadn't wanted a big do, and neither had Rafael.

They were happy as they were, living quietly, with Rafael commuting to Palermo for work. Allegra had started offering cello lessons to local children, and enjoyed playing more than she ever had. The local priest had asked her to play a concert in the church in the nearby town, and Allegra had agreed.

Love, she realised, made her bloom. Made her believe more in herself, because Rafael believed in her. And she saw the same unfurling in Rafael, the lightness and sheer joy in his face, his eyes. Love made you bloom and love also healed.

In recent months Rafael had taken new steps with Angelica, talking more honestly to her than he ever had before. Last week Angelica had moved into the clinic in Switzerland and was undergoing several months of rehab and therapy. So many miracles.

'Allegra, look!' His voice filled with amazement, Rafael pointed to their son who, with a look of both determination and terror on his face, was taking his first step.

'He's amazing,' Rafael declared, and, laughing, Allegra reached out to clasp Marco's hands.

'Just like his father, then,' she said, and, smiling, Rafael leaned down to kiss her.

\* \* \* \* \*

*If you enjoyed*
*ENGAGED FOR HER ENEMY'S HEIR,*
*why not explore these other*
ONE NIGHT WITH CONSEQUENCES
*themed stories?*

*A RING FOR THE GREEK'S BABY*
*by Melanie Milburne*
*THE PREGNANT KAVAKOS BRIDE*
*by Sharon Kendrick*
*THE BOSS'S NINE-MONTH NEGOTIATION*
*by Maya Blake*
*THE CONSEQUENCE OF HIS VEN-*
*GEANCE*
*by Jennie Lucas*
*A CHILD CLAIMED BY GOLD*
*by Rachael Thomas*

*Available now!*